THE SONS OF BITCHES HAD
COME FOR HIM...

Raider shifted forward a few feet, moving in what he hoped was silence, and lay flat on the hard boards, facing the door and aiming the deadly shotgun straight down the hallway beyond it.

If anyone was in that hall when the door sprang open...

The kitchen door burst wide, flying back on its hinges and rebounding against the wall.

Raider triggered the first barrel, and a scythe of hot lead chopped into the bodies of the two men in the hallway.

Both went down screaming, but Raider had no time to think about them now.

He rolled, bringing the squat, ugly muzzles of the shotgun away from the hall and toward the porch...

Other books in the *RAIDER* series by
J. D. HARDIN

RAIDER

THE GULF
PIRATES

J.D. HARDIN

B

BERKLEY BOOKS, NEW YORK

THE GULF PIRATES

A Berkley Book/published by arrangement with
the author

PRINTING HISTORY
Berkley editon/March 1988

ISBN: 0-425-10702-7

CHAPTER ONE

The fat man stood and extended his hand, but he was not particularly cordial about it. If anything he looked dubious.

"You are, uh, Mr. Raider?"

"That's right."

"Of the, uh, Pinkerton Detective Agency?" He acted like he rather hoped there was more than one Raider in the neighborhood and that the one he wanted would turn out to be the other Raider.

Raider smiled at him. "That's right. Mind if I sit down?"

"Oh. Yes. Go right ahead. Smoke?"

"No."

The fat man was smoking a short stub of chubby cigar. The smell of it was vile, but the man was entitled to whatever vices he wanted in his own office.

"Yes. Well." The fat man rubbed his hands together and looked Raider over carefully.

Raider knew what the man was seeing. Not impressive in the world of business, for sure. Slick clothing and sweet-smelling hair tonics were not exactly what Raider went in for. Instead Raider was tall and lean, with a horseman's narrow hips and a workingman's breadth of shoulder. He was dark. Black hair and a sweep of black mustache. Black eyes hooded by his Stetson hat. He wore a leather coat old enough and scuffed enough to be considered disreputable in some circles —particularly in the fancy surroundings of this office—faded jeans, and boots that needed the heels replaced. In fact, about the only article he had on that looked like it was in good condition was the Remington revolver that rode at his waist.

And the fat man looked like that blued and oiled steel item bothered him. His eyes kept cutting toward it and darting away again like he didn't want Raider to know that he was uncomfortable with firearms.

Raider smiled and made it easier for the fat man. "Mr. Bell, I was told you wanted an investigator to help you with a problem. Not some young executive who might want to marry your daughter. Pinkerton operatives are required to travel in places where you might not be comfortable going, sir. And that's what I can do. Naturally, if you want somebody with a better tailor for this job, I'm sure the agency can find someone more suited to your needs."

Bell looked embarrassed. "No. Not at all. I uh . . . your reputation is excellent, Mr. Raider. Excellent. That is why I . . . we . . . were pleased that you were available."

"Thank you." Raider settled back in the leather-upholstered office chair, content to let Bell stew if he wanted to. Fat men are supposed to be jolly, but this Morton Bell fellow was a long way from being that. He was a nervous type, his vest gaping between the buttons from the size of his belly, and his graying hair thinning on top. Give him a few more years, Raider thought, and the poor man would be bald, dyspeptic, and fat to boot. The man probably earned thirty times Raider's salary, and Raider envied him not at all.

"You, uh, have been informed of our problem, Mr. Raider?" Bell asked.

"Nope." There was more Raider could have added to that. Allan Pinkerton's legendary parsimony was a fact. The agency spent no more on telegrams than was absolutely necessary. The message that reached Raider told him only that he was to report to a Mr. Morton Bell at the Gulf Insurance Company, Mobile, Alabama, without delay. The telegram hadn't even given the address of Gulf's office building. Raider had had to learn that after he arrived in the old city on the bay.

Morton Bell, who turned out to be Gulf Insurance's vice-president in charge of something or other, wrung his hands again. "I see." He ground his cigar out in an ashtray large enough to require two men to lift the thing. Or so it looked, anyway. Helluva deal for the cleaning lady, no doubt.

The man seemed unsure how he should proceed.

"Mr. Bell, why don't you just tell me what your problem

is. Right from the beginning. Then we'll see if I can help you with it."

"Yes, uh . . . of course." The fat man nibbled at his underlip for a moment. "There are, uh, considerations here that are . . . beyond the scope of our normal business considerations, you see."

In fact, Raider did not see. Yet.

"My advice, quite frankly, has been from the outset that we should simply cancel the, uh, outstanding policies. Wash our hands of the affair, so to speak. That advice has not, uh, been accepted. Our founder and chairman of the board has over-ruled that judgment." He smiled as if he really believed he had just explained something. "And that, sir, is why we deter-mined to employ the Pinkerton Detective Agency."

"But, Mr. Bell. What is the *problem*?"

The Gulf Insurance Company was a specialist in marine insur-ance, writing policies against ships and cargoes plying the Gulf of Mexico, the Caribbean Sea, and, in recent years, the transatlantic trade as well. The company had been in business for twenty-two eminently successful years, moving to Mobile some twenty years earlier after a shaky start in the hide, tal-low, and lumber trade along the Gulf coast of south Texas.

The fledgling company was begun with more guts than capital by Emmett Maxwell. Maxwell would have foundered on the shoals of competition from New Orleans insurors ex-cept for the faith, the policy, and most important the premium fees paid by a Gulf coast shipowner named Jon Harwig. Max-well was grateful to Harwig for all the successes that followed the early, impoverished start. Now Harwig was in trouble. Maxwell felt an obligation to his first and oldest policyholder and wanted to bail the man out of trouble, but Bell's judgment was that the longstanding policies should be canceled and Harwig's small fleet be allowed to sink—figuratively speak-ing, that is—without taking Gulf Insurance Company's profits with them.

"The problem, you see . . ."

At last we're getting to it, Raider thought, his expression showing nothing but patience and polite attention.

". . . is that this Harwig's ships and cargoes keep disap-pearing. Piracy, they claim."

For the first time Raider felt a stirring of genuine interest. "Piracy? In this day and age?"

Bell sighed. His mouth twisted into a sour expression of distaste and barely concealed disbelief. "Piracy," he confirmed.

"All right. Piracy it is."

Bell grimaced. It was plain that he doubted the story he was required to pass along to the Pinkerton operative. "To date, sir, we have settled claims for the disappearance of five ships and four insured cargoes."

"The fifth cargo wasn't insured?"

"The fifth ship was riding empty except for ballast. It is my understanding that the Harwig Line is finding it, um, difficult to obtain cargo. For obvious reasons."

Raider nodded. "Your company pays them back for the losses, but they've already lost whatever they were shipping. And somebody needs that stuff, whatever it is, or they wouldn't bother shipping it. Right?"

"Precisely," Bell said.

Raider fingered his chin. "Just at first glance, Mr. Bell, I'd've thought this would be a matter for the Navy to look into. Or whoever it is that looks into such things."

"Inquiries have been made. Crew members from each of the Harwig Line ships have been interviewed. On the basis of those formal inquiries, a finding of loss due to piracy on the high seas has been issued. Formally, that is. In private... well, I believe the Navy leans in the same direction I do, Mr. Raider."

"And that is?"

"Insurance fraud, Mr. Raider. Plain and simple. I believe Mr. Harwig is defrauding and deluding a fine, fine gentleman who believes in him."

Raider smiled. "What it comes down to, Mr. Bell, is that Gulf Insurance wants the Pinkerton Agency to find the pirates, but Morton Bell wants *me* to unmask Jon Harwig as the pirate."

For the first time since Raider entered his office the fat man looked genuinely pleased. "You did not hear me say that, Mr. Raider."

"No, of course I didn't, Mr. Bell."

Bell made his way out of his chair, having to use his hands on his desk top for leverage, and turned toward a shiny, polished teakwood cabinet against the side wall. "May I offer you a drink, sir?"

"My pleasure, Mr. Bell."

"Then we can go downstairs. I assume you will want to see our files on the Harwig Line. Those can give you all the details."

"That will be fine," Raider said.

"I like you, Mr. Raider."

"Thank you," Raider said, neglecting to return the compliment since he was not yet quite so sure about Morton Bell, vice-president in charge of something or other for the Gulf Insurance Company. He did, though, accept a glass of ancient and truly excellent bourbon from the fat man.

"To your health, sir," Morton Bell said, raising his glass.

CHAPTER TWO

Raider stood, hands in his pockets, leaning against a pile of burlap-wrapped cotton bales. The scene before him was as fascinating as it was unfamiliar. Longshoremen were sweating and straining to unload cotton from a seemingly endless chain of wagons, while a few yards away a tubby, fat-waisted cargo ship was being warped into the pier—wharf? jetty? Raider wasn't entirely sure what the thing should be called—with heavy cables of braided hemp. A boom operator was already rigging the cargo nets and tackle that would lift the huge bales of cotton aboard the ship. The sailors Raider could see on the deck of the ship looked bored. But then they were already familiar with the process. Raider was much more accustomed to cow towns and mountains and deserts.

"Is that the *Henrietta?*" Raider asked a passerby who was trying to refer to a sheaf of papers in his hand and walk through a maze of ropes and cables at the same time.

"Huh?" The man stopped and blinked.

"I asked if that would be the *Henrietta,*" Raider repeated.

"Her? Hell no, mister. Look for a floating slop bucket—that'll be the *Henrietta.*" The man hurried on about his business, scarcely taking the time to look at the stranger but at least polite enough to give an answer.

Raider grunted and went back to his observations.

He had been to New Orleans before, of course, but he had never paid all that much attention to the waterfront—except, perhaps, for some of the dives where the seamen partied.

Now, two days and one train ride after his meeting with Morton Bell in Mobile, Raider had good reason to take inter-

7

est in the shipping traffic here. According to the insuror's records, confirmed by a cargo agent representing the Harwig Line, the *Harwig Henrietta* was due to call at New Orleans from Cedar Key, en route to Galveston, Port Lavaca, and Rockport. Raider intended to take passage on the *Henrietta*.

He had been frankly a bit excited about the prospect of a sea voyage when he was making the slow, sooty train trip over from Mobile.

Visions of tall ships kept running through his thoughts, sleek giants with their masts straining toward the sky, sails billowing full to the breeze. The great clippers of the China trade. Something like that.

He laughed softly to himself. The ships he could see in port right now were mostly scabrous, wallowing things with mildewed, much-patched sails and riggings that were a spiderweb maze of confusion to a landsman like Raider.

Picture-book clippers they were not. Not the best of them.

The ship he had been watching was brought up against the fenders at the side of the wooden pier—that term would have to do for lack of knowledge on the subject—and secured. Almost before the motion of the ship was stopped, the hatches were dragged open and the boom operator was lifting the first net of bales over the deck from dockside, positioning the load with an intriguing degree of delicacy and quickly paying out cable to lower the cotton into the hold of the ship.

These boys knew what they were doing, Raider reflected.

But this was not the *Henrietta*. He walked on, ambling like a tourist along the wharves and piers, stopping now and then to ask directions. No one seemed to know exactly where the *Harwig Henrietta* was, but everyone had a guess as to where she might be. Following one speculation after another gave Raider a thorough look at the activity on the New Orleans waterfront. Riverfront, he guessed it really was here. Water, anyhow, complete with floating debris and waterlogged refuse that he not only did not recognize but did not want to—not judging by the smells coming off the water here.

"The *Henrietta*?" he asked a black boy of twelve or thirteen who was wandering through the crowd with a black-painted box slung from his shoulder on a scrap of rope.

"Wanna buy a crab cake, mister? Best crab cakes in N'Orleans," the boy offered with a grin.

"How much?"

"Two for a nickel, mister."

"Tell you what, son, I'll buy two of them. For a dime. If you'll show me where the *Henrietta* is."

The child's grin got even bigger. He opened the lid of his box and selected a pair of plump, crumb-coated fried crab cakes. Raider handed over the promised dime, and the boy laughed.

"That's her, mister. Right there." The ship in question was tied up not forty yards from where they were standing. The boy hesitated for a moment. "You ain't mad, are you, mister?"

"No, I ain't mad." Raider tipped the kid another nickel and got a flashing grin and a happy thank-you in return.

Munching the crab cakes—they were hot, greasy, and marvelous—Raider moved closer to the *Henrietta* to take a look at her.

He had quite frankly overlooked the little ship before because he had assumed that anything this size must be a river runner, incapable of handling the open seas.

The *Henrietta* couldn't have been more than forty-five or fifty feet long, very wide at the waist, and squatly ungainly in appearance.

Look for a floating slop bucket, the man had said. Now Raider could understand what the fellow meant. The *Henrietta* looked about as sturdily built as your average bathtub. And not a hell of a lot bigger next to the other ships on the busy waterfront. The scruffy thing also looked as if no one had bothered to paint her in decades. Even Raider's untrained eye could see that the *Henrietta* was a mess compared to the other ships.

And this was the ship he would trust his life to on the way to Rockport.

He hoped they at least had some lifeboats aboard that would float. It wouldn't surprise him any if the small boats were needed before the voyage was over.

Still, the *Henrietta* was a Harwig ship, and he intended to travel the Harwig Line.

He turned away from the unimpressive sight of his soon-to-be temporary home and made his way toward the ticket agents's kiosks that were bunched together on the landward side of the waterfront. One of them would surely have the *Henrietta* posted for sailing. His intention was to buy passage without letting on to anyone that he was a Pinkerton operative.

CHAPTER THREE

The *Henrietta* reached open water and spread her sails with a great flapping and snapping of canvas. The boat—the thing was too damn small for Raider to think of it as a ship, no matter what anybody said—heeled over, and Raider staggered sideways for a moment until he spread his legs wide and righted himself. He wasn't entirely sure he was going to like this sea voyage shit.

"Feeling queasy already?" the first mate asked.

"Nope." It wasn't a lie. Not exactly. He didn't want to puke. He just felt a little hollow in the belly. Nothing serious so far.

The seaman grinned at him and went on about his business, which mostly seemed to consist of standing with his feet planted wide and a pipe between his teeth while he shouted orders freely mixed with curses at the sailors who were pulling on ropes and running back and forth and cranking winches and doing whatever the hell it was they were supposed to do.

As far as Raider could see it was all just so much confusion. But he seemed to be the only one aboard who thought so.

Already this business of sailoring was looking mighty unattractive to a man who was accustomed to the feel of a good horse between his knees. Or a good woman around them. There were a dozen crew members on the *Henrietta* and one passenger, and every one of them had their equipment hanging down between their legs. Not a female in the lot.

"How long to Rockport?" Raider asked the nearest sailor.

The man gave him a vacant smile and a shrug.

Whenever. Apparently that was close enough for these men who lived at the whim of the winds and the currents.

Raider frowned and walked forward along the cluttered deck.

This wasn't exactly the way he had envisioned it. Not only had his imagined images of tall, stately clipper ships been shattered by the sluggish, wallowy *Henrietta*, it didn't *feel* the way it was supposed to either.

Somehow he'd always figured that standing in the prow of a ship at sea would be something like riding a smooth-gaited horse: standing proud, with the bow slicing through the waves and the wind of speed in your face.

Why, hell, this tub was rolling and thrashing and shoving its way through the water. And the wind wasn't in his face at all. It was coming from behind, and not very strong at that. Just a breeze. But then that kind of made sense. They were going with the wind and moving in the same direction it was, so now that he thought about it, of course it couldn't be in his face or they'd be sailing backward. Damn, but this just wasn't the way he had thought it would be.

And locked on board this moving bathtub without so much as the sight of a woman until they got there. Whenever that was.

He shook his head and tried to concentrate on the job that lay ahead.

Bell had showed him the insurance company records on the Harwig Line. All their ships, their cargoes, and in particular their recent spate of losses.

It took no particular skill to spot the patterns in the losses. No clue in that, of course, about whether they were really dealing with pirates here, but the pattern was clear enough.

Five ships and four cargoes paid off by the insurors, and every one of those losses at the home-port end of the voyages.

Every one of the losses taking place within a hundred sea miles of Rockport on the Gulf coast of Texas.

Every one of them close to home.

And interestingly enough, every Harwig Line crew member safe and hale afterward.

Not a man had been lost or so much as harmed.

Three times the crew had been taken close to shore and deposited safely in lifeboats to make their way home.

Twice the crew had been taken all the way to firm ground

by the pirates and let off on Matagorda Island, where they had to signal fishermen for their final rescue.

Reports from the Navy's investigations, also on file in the insurance company records, gave detail to only a little more knowledge.

The crew members all said that, yup, they were taken by pirates, all right. The ships and cargoes had been stolen, all right. Beyond that no one seemed to know a hell of a lot.

Raider couldn't help but wonder if the sailors were loyal enough to lie for Jon Harwig. Like if for instance he was scuttling—or even quietly selling—his own boats and leaning on the insurance company for his profits. If Harwig asked them to lie, would they?

Before he left Mobile Raider had gone through the crew and witness lists. One sailor had been on three of the lost ships. An officer listed as a bosun, whatever that was, was listed twice. Between the two repeat victims they had sailed on only four of the lost ships, though, so there might or might not have been particular significance to their being on the crew lists.

It was something Raider would have to check out, but somehow he doubted there would be anything to it.

He looked around. The wind had shifted slightly or else the *Henrietta* was steering to a new angle, so that the wind was coming more from his left now than from behind and the sailors were jumping to change the angle of the sails.

The oily, green-gray waters around them were empty all the way to the low, barely seen shoreline off to the right.

There wasn't another ship anywhere in sight.

How in hell a bunch of pirates could suddenly pop up out of nowhere and capture another vessel was something Raider couldn't figure.

The official reports of the supposed piracy had said that the pirates boarded and took the Harwig ships. But none of the reports went into much detail about just how the pirates were supposed to have accomplished such a thing.

This wasn't, after all, like an Indian attack. Couldn't have been an ambush sort of thing. Hell, where does a man hide on open water? There weren't any hillocks or bushes to hide behind. There weren't any roads that a ship had to follow either. A ship could wander just any damn place it pleased. Why, a pirate wouldn't know where to hide even if he could figure out a way to do it.

It didn't make sense to Raider, just as it obviously didn't make any sense to Morton Bell back in Mobile. Maybe the man was right about Jon Harwig arranging piracy for his own convenience.

Still, it was way too early to be making that kind of conclusion. And a man who already has his mind made up isn't going to learn very much when he goes about trying to conduct an investigation.

A man who already thinks he has the answers will only be looking for things to support his notions, not for real facts. Likely he'll be blind to the things that don't fit what he expects to find. So better to know that kind of thinking right now before it could get a foothold.

"Mr. Raider?"

The tall Pinkerton turned to see the cabin boy, a youngster in his late teens, who knuckled the front of his knitted watch cap in a salute of sorts. "Yes?"

"Cap'n wants to know would you wanta join him for lunch, sir."

Raider's stomach roiled and objected to the thought of food. Not that he was seasick. Exactly. He just didn't want to eat anything right now.

"I think I'll pass, thanks."

"Yes, sir," the cabin boy said politely, with only the merest hint of a smile giving a clue to what he was really thinking.

The breeze shifted again and the *Henrietta* lurched and wallowed, and Raider had to grab the railing for support. The cabin boy trotted away toward the aft cabins as if he hadn't so much as noticed.

"I hope this is gonna be a short trip," Raider muttered under his breath.

CHAPTER FOUR

Raider saw little of Galveston. Instead of going to the bother —and the expense—of docking at the sprawling, gray-weathered port, Captain Mason anchored well out from the quay amid a dozen other small ships and hailed a lighter to discharge the few crates consigned there.

It seemed foolish to make an extra port call for three wooden boxes of no great size, but none of the crew seemed to think it unusual. And perhaps it wasn't. Raider didn't know half enough, he was beginning to suspect, about the workings of ships and freight and pirates to know if this stop at Galveston would be considered normal or if it was a sign of how desperate Harwig was for trade that he would accept payment of the few pennies so tiny a cargo might bring in.

So far on the voyage from New Orleans, no one in Raider's hearing had mentioned anything about pirates or Harwig losses. Raider had been careful to avoid bringing it up himself. Better to eavesdrop than to question at this point, he decided, when no one aboard except himself knew his real purpose in sailing with the Harwig Line.

At least by now he was becoming more comfortable with the ship and its motion. He was able to eat with some degree of pleasure and, more important, to hold down what he had eaten. His first few meals on the *Henrietta* went overboard shortly after their consumption.

The first mate—called Mr. McInally by everyone from the captain on down—came to stand beside Raider while the Galveston freight was being unloaded into the lighter under the direction of Second Mate Forrest.

"Having a pleasant journey, are ye, Mr. Raider?"

"Better lately than it was to begin with. Though I suppose you wouldn't know about such things."

McInally laughed. "Well enough do I remember it, sar. First shipped as a lad, an' it was four months before I could stand nor hold down more'n a crust o' dry bread." He laughed again. "Four more afore me backside went back t' normal too, I tell ye."

Raider was not entirely sure if the crusty sailor was joking him or not. He decided not to play the greenhorn and bite, anyway. Likely McInally was opening a door and inviting him in for a ribbing, much the same way a cowboy trail crew will scare an Easterner wide-eyed with tales of snakes and tornadoes and wild, wild Indians.

"Will we be long into Rockport, Mr. McInally?"

The first mate tamped black, long-cut tobacco into the huge bowl of his pipe and struck a match to it before he answered. "That's a matter ye'll have t' take up with a higher authority than I, Mr. Raider. An' I'm not speakin' of the captain, sir. We arrive when we arrive, at the will o' Naptune an' the winds an' the fates." He puffed on his pipe for a moment. "With the wind fair, sir, an' no interference, we should be there in five days, allowin' one for a stop at Lavaca."

"Interference, Mr. McInally? What kind of interference could there be on a calm, open sea?"

McInally turned to look out into the Gulf. "There's things a land dweller canna know, Mr. Raider. Storms, pirates . . ." He winked. "There's even those as say there's giant serpents lives beneath the green waters. Serpents big enou' to wrap its ten'acles around a ship an' drag 'er to the bottom with all hands still aboard."

Raider was not sure if he was expected to laugh now or not. The seaman certainly was managing to sound serious about it. "Serpents I've no belief in, Mr. McInally, and the weather looks fair enough. But surely you can't be telling me there are still pirates. Not in this day and age."

"Aye, pirates indeed, Mr. Raider. In this day an' age. Why let me tell you a thing or two . . ."

He did, relating another version of the piracy Raider was here to investigate.

As far as McInally was concerned, the cargoes might never have been taken. He didn't mention anything about those losses. But the loss of the ships seemed painful to him even though they were another man's ships.

"Surely a man couldn't expect to steal a ship and profit from it," Raider protested. "What would he do with it? Where could he hide it? People who have seen a ship before and are familiar with it, surely those same men would be sailing everywhere a small ship could reach. Surely someone would recognize one of the stolen ships."

It was a point that had been gnawing at him since he read Bell's files. Theft has profit as its motive. And surely a seaman could recognize a ship he has known before regardless of changes of paint or name, just like a cattleman can recognize the hundreds of individual cows that may be in his herd or a miner know his own set of drills.

"Ah, you've struck on it sure, Mr. Raider. That's a thing as has been botherin' me since this piracy begun, sir. I know I an' every lad of my acquaintance has been looking for them lost ships, but never a glimmer, sir. Never a glimmer. Surely one of us shoulda seen somethin' e'en was they refitted and sold below the border. Goods a man could thieve an' sell, but a ship is a live thing an' calls out to her own. Yet I've not heard a breath about any of 'em, and believe me, sar, I've asked."

"It's a puzzlement," Raider agreed.

"An' so it is, sar." The man puffed on his pipe again. His attention was on the lighter, which was pulling away toward the busy Galveston wharf now, and on the men of the *Henrietta* who were clearing the slings and replacing the hatch covers.

" 'Scuse me, Mr. Raider." McInally hurried away to give orders for getting under way again.

As far as Raider could tell, Captain Mason mostly ate well, drank well, and belched occasionally, while First Mate McInally did most of the day-to-day running of the ship. There was no sign of Mason on deck now, nor did McInally seem to need the captain's guidance.

Raider looked for an out-of-the-way spot. The crew was dashing madly about again as they set the sails and pointed southwest.

CHAPTER FIVE

The stop at Port Lavaca took longer but otherwise was no more interesting than the call at Galveston. At Lavaca they had to tie up at a rickety pier and rig booms to haul several large crates out of the hold, and most of a day was consumed with the unloading of green cedar lumber from a forward hold. The *Henrietta* rode considerably higher when they were done, and Raider suspected that the remainder of the trip downcoast to Rockport would be uncomfortable with so much less weight below decks. The already wallowy little ship would likely bob like a cork in a pail now.

Raider asked one of the sailors about his suspicions.

"Aye, we'd take ballast 'cause of it," the young, sun-bronzed man confirmed, "except from here we can hide inside the island the whole rest o' the way."

Raider lifted an eyebrow.

The sailor pointed out to sea. "Inland passage over there. Runs inside o' Matagorda Island, y' see." He grinned. "Easy passage now, mister." Raider's early discomfort was—could have been—no secret on the tiny vessel.

"Thanks."

The *Henrietta* laid over at Port Lavaca that night. When Raider left the ship for an evening ashore, with a meal taken at a table where the forks and spoons remained where you laid them, without sliding back and forth from the movement of the ship, he was warned to be back aboard early. "We sail on the morning tide."

True to that word, the lines were slipped before dawn, the sailing from port controlled not by the sun but by the tides,

19

and the *Henrietta* crabbed slowly away from the pier into an offshore breeze.

As usual Raider stood well out of the way and watched the sailors at work. Simple observation was bringing some small sense of order out of the seeming confusion, and he could see now that Benny was setting a jib while Gunter was trimming the main sheets and the cabin boy was standing forward with a lead-weighted line held ready to take soundings. Even Mason was on deck, although once again it was McInally who was actually giving the orders.

"A fine morning, Mr. Raider," Mason said.

"Yes," he agreed, but turned his coat collar up against the chill of the predawn air. The first hint of light was just beginning to show a pale line beneath the clouds far out in the Gulf.

"You look worried, Mr. Raider."

"Not really. It's just—"

The captain of the *Henrietta* threw his hand back and laughed. After a single night on firm ground, Raider was once again feeling his stomach rebel at the slow rolling of the nearly empty ship.

"Not to worry, Mr. Raider. We'll be inside the protection of Matagorda soon. Be light enough by the time we reach her, and the wind is fair."

"If you say so," Raider said unhappily. He suspected he was in danger of losing whatever remained from a good steak and a quantity of decent whiskey. Fortunately, the rest of last night's pleasures could not be taken away from him, except perhaps for a lingering hint of perfume that clung to his limp shirt.

Mason chuckled and ambled forward to say something to his first mate. Raider stuffed his hands deep in his pockets and concentrated on thinking about the beauty of the morning— the clean, salt tang that spiced the air here, the growing color in the clouds off to the east, the half-seen soaring of gulls already out in search of whatever it was gulls searched for— trying to think about almost anything, in fact, except the monotonous, gut-wrenching rolling of the *Henrietta*.

He felt much better after the ship finally heeled slowly to the right and slid into the broad channel between the dunes of Matagorda Island and the flat, ugly terrain of the mainland. At least then the *Henrietta* established a straight and easy course through protected waters, and the wallowing blessedly quit.

"There's more traffic than we've seen before," Raider observed.

"Fisherfolk with their wee boats an' silly nets," McInally said. There was a hint of condescension and perhaps even contempt in his voice when he said it. Probably, Raider suspected, the same tone that an officer on a whaler or Horn-rounding clipper would use when referring to anyone on the Gulf-locked *Henrietta*.

"Pretty, though," Raider said. He meant it. The pale triangles of sail were handsome in the slanting light of late afternoon.

"Pretty enough," McInally agreed. "Not fit to face real water, though. Shallow-draft li'l things suitable to the making of pennies." He winked. "Or to carryin' the pretty ladies for a Sunday picnic on th' islands, eh?"

Raider smiled. Although his limited experience with the water made him sure that a buggy and bay horse, not a small boat and a bay, were by far the better way to take a young lady on an outing.

"Fast, some of 'em, though," McInally said, this time with a note of approval in his tone. "Look at all the sail that'un has set."

Raider looked in the direction McInally was pointing. Yet another of the innumerable small boats had come out of an inlet and was cutting handsomely through the water at a spanking clip. Raider didn't know enough about seamanship to judge the amount of sail the small craft was carrying, but even he could see how far to the right—to starboard, he remembered—the slender craft was heeled.

Several of her crew members, laughing, dark-tanned young men, were leaning their weight out over the gunwale to counterweight the thrust of the wind against their boat. They looked like they were having fun, Raider thought.

The little boat cut through the water at easily twice the speed of the ponderous *Henrietta*, overtaking them from the rear.

"That lad at the tiller's no seaman," McInally observed. He

reached into a pocket and produced his pipe and pouch. "Lovely boat, though, eh?"

"Why do you say he's not a sailor?" Raider asked.

"See how he's keepin' 'er to lee'ard. Soon as they come beneath us, our sails'll rob 'is wind, and he'll lose way."

The handsome little boat was close behind them now, moving like a thoroughbred colt beside a plow horse. The sporty craft came within twenty yards or so of the *Henrietta*'s stern, then suddenly veered hard to her left.

"Ah! He sees 'is mistake now," McInally said with satisfaction. He scraped a match aflame and applied it carefully to his pipe, then explained to Raider, "He'll do better t' overtake us t' larboard."

"Which means he'll rob our wind, right?"

McInally smiled. "Aye, Mr. Raider, ye're learning. Why, we'll make a seaman o' you yet. Though in truth, sar, a li'l thang like that, we'll scarce notice th' breeze he captures. An' it harms us none if he took it all for the moment it'll take 'im to get by."

The small boat passed close under the high stern of the *Henrietta*, so that for a moment the hull and laughing crew of the little craft were hidden from sight and all Raider could see of the boat was the upper half of the sails, flapping slightly— they had told him that was called luffing; damned silly to try and remember when it only meant flapping—as the craft came too high into the wind.

The small boat hesitated there for an instant—more of the inexperience of the man at the tiller, Raider suspected—then once again fell off to capture the thrust of the wind and surged forward, this time a few yards farther behind the *Henrietta* but angled nicely to pass close to the upwind side of the tubby freight ship.

"Handsome. Damned handsome," Raider said.

"Aye, she is." McInally puffed on his pipe. He and the rest of the crew on deck were admiring the light, swift motion of the boat beside them.

The boat drew alongside, staying just far enough away to keep her starboard-heeled sails from fouling the rigging of the *Henrietta*—Raider almost could have reached out and grabbed hold of the smaller boat's mainsail—then inexplicably slowed, her crew letting the mainsail out to spill air until the little craft was pacing handily at the *Henrietta*'s side and matching the larger vessel's slow speed.

Raider and everyone else above deck on the *Henrietta* were at the port rail watching.

A middle-aged man came into view. The small boat's crew had been hidden by the sails. Now the mustached man ducked under the boom to the lee side of his own mainsail and cupped his hands around his mouth so he could hail the *Henrietta*.

"Is Cap'n Mason there?"

"The cap'n is below," McInally shouted back. "I be the first officer. Can I be o' service, sar?"

The man standing a good dozen feet lower than the deck of the *Henrietta* laughed. "Aye, Mr. McInally. If you would be good enough to look behind you, sir, you will find that your vessel has been taken. Be good enough, sir, to inform your crew that they will come to no harm."

Raider's head snapped back toward the stern, where now three men—three sailors—stood with Colt revolving shotguns leveled.

The sons of bitches must somehow have come aboard when the small boat was slicing under the stern of the *Henrietta*.

Raider frowned. Reflexively his hand moved toward the butt of the Remington that rode as always on his gunbelt.

McInally stopped him with a light touch on his elbow. "Please don't, sar. The boy is in danger."

Raider hadn't noticed a very pale, very frightened-looking cabin boy crouched cowering under the shotgun muzzle of the pirate on the far left.

Pirate. Because that, by damn, was exactly what these SOBs were.

"Steady as you go," the pirate chieftain hailed from the deck of his small, fast craft beside them.

"Steady as ye go," McInally repeated for his crew.

The pirate craft slipped more wind and began dropping back beside the slowly moving *Henrietta*. Raider could see a pirate crewman come to the narrow, pointed bow of the small boat with a coiled line in his hands, and one of the pirates on board the *Henrietta* set his shotgun aside to trot aft, ready to receive the line from below.

"Shit!" Raider muttered between tightly clenched teeth.

On the other hand, this sure as hell answered the question about whether there really were any pirates involved in the Harwig Line's troubles. Of course it still remained to be seen who was behind *them*.

"Shit," he said again, having to restrain himself from reaching for his Remington.

CHAPTER SIX

There were six of the pirates, three who had come aboard at the stern of the *Henrietta* and three who had stayed to handle the small boat until it was secured behind the freighter and they could all come onto the larger ship.

Funny thing how pretty the pirate vessel still was, Raider thought. He had always had a mental image of pirate ships being ugly, looming things bristling with cannon and Jolly Roger flags. The reality of this one was a sleek and attractive sailboat that looked as though it should be a pleasure yacht.

Well, this was no pleasure.

"It's about that gun you're wearing," the pirate captain said when he was aboard the *Henrietta*. "We would be obliged if you would hand it over." The man was polite. And sounded very much in control of himself, his men, and this ship.

Raider smiled at him, although there was no hint of humor in the expression. "For the sake of the crew I'll be willing to put it in my bag. But if you want me to give it up to you, mister, you'll have to be man enough to take it."

If the pirate was armed, his weapons were damned well concealed. The threat came from the revolving shotguns, five of them now that all the pirates were aboard, each one of which could spew death across the decks of the *Henrietta*.

The pirate captain considered Raider's refusal for a moment, then relaxed. "Boy, go below and get the gentleman's bag."

The cabin boy seemed positively relieved to be able to scuttle out from under the threat of the shotgun muzzles. He took off at a scampering run and was back within moments carrying Raider's Gladstone.

Reluctantly, with at least three of the repeating shotguns trained on him, Raider removed his gunbelt and deposited it inside the bag. Then he buckled the retaining straps in place over the closed bag. There would be no fast draws out of that arrangement, damn it.

"Thank you," the new captain of the *Henrietta* said. "We have no interest in the theft of personal valuables. Only this ship and its cargo. Each of you is free to go below—one at a time so there is no temptation, mind you—and get anything you wish to take off with you." He motioned to Captain Mason, who stiffened his back and shook his head.

"I'll not be leaving my ship," Mason declared.

"Please, Captain," the pirate said. "No trouble, now. It's your men who would suffer, sir. I would feel compelled to see to that."

Mason squared his shoulders but nodded. "For the sake of my crew, sir."

Raider would almost have sworn that Mason was not a party to this piracy. The seaman looked thoroughly pissed. No one who made his living from the sea could have been that good an actor too. Hell, he could have made his fortune on the stage if he were capable of that much deception.

"Gather your things, then, sir," the pirate captain said agreeably. "You may take the log if you wish."

Mason nodded again and marched stiffly away.

The *Henrietta* continued to sail slowly south through the inland passage between Matagorda Island and the mainland.

The pirate captain motioned for the crew of the *Henrietta* to gather forward, and one of his men set his shotgun aside to assume control of the rudder.

"No tricks, gentlemen. We mean you no harm, understand. We only want the ship."

"Considerate SOB, ain't you," Raider said loud enough for all to hear. Being held up at gunpoint, regardless of the sur-roundings, was not his notion of a good time, and he was getting madder the more he thought about it. If only . . . The hell with that. Wishes don't change facts worth a damn, and the plain fact was that they *were* being held up at gunpoint, like it or not.

The pirate captain didn't seem to mind the name-calling in

the slightest. He gave Raider a tolerantly amused look and asked, "And who would you be, sir?"

"A passenger," Raider said.

"My apologies for the delay in your journey and for any inconvenience," the man said gallantly. He gave Raider a slight, ironic bow and smiled.

"You two," he said to two of the *Henrietta*'s crew. "Make sure this gentleman's gear is all transferred to the *Cockleshell*, if you please."

The *Cockleshell*, Raider guessed, would be the small pirate boat.

"What are your intentions?" Raider demanded.

"Why, no harm whatsoever, sir," the pirate captain said. "We shall transfer any personal possessions to the *Cockleshell* and ask you to go your own way." He smiled again. "After, that is, opening the seacock. We wouldn't want you following, would we? And the craft really should be returned to its rightful owner. A lovely boat, the *Cockleshell*. We shouldn't want her to come to permanent harm. A new seacock will make her right again. Call it, um, fifteen, sixteen dollars for the replacement. You, Mr. McInally. Here." He beckoned the first mate closer, then reached in his pocket and pulled out a double eagle. "See to it that the owner of the boat receives this, eh? Small payment for the trouble involved but"—he shrugged—"one does what one can."

McInally seemed in no better a humor about his than Mason was. He jammed the coin into his pocket and angrily knocked the dottle of his pipe out on the rail of the *Henrietta*, spilling ash and a live coal into the water below.

Mason reappeared on deck, dragging a sea bag behind him and carrying an oilcloth-wrapped bundle tight against his chest. Raider guessed that the preciously held bundle would contain the *Henrietta*'s log and perhaps Mason's navigation instruments. Sailors, he had already noticed, seemed to regard such things as being of value much beyond their obvious worth.

"You next, Mr. McInally," the pirate captain ordered.

The first mate went aft and below, down to the cabins given to the use of ships's officers and any passengers. The ordinary sailors had quarters forward, a part of the *Henrietta* where Raider had never been.

Raider hoped all this was not a charade. Certainly past

experience indicated that crewmen on the captured ships would not be harmed. Still, he couldn't help but notice that none of the pirates, from their captain on down, showed any inclination to cover his face to protect himself from future recognition.

And he noticed too that the men holding the shotguns seemed entirely competent in the way they handled the weapons.

The proof of that pudding would come when the *Henrietta*'s crew was ready to transfer to the *Cockleshell*.

Raider began to wish he were carrying a hideout gun, but he wasn't, and his Remington was securely fastened away inside the awkward damned Gladstone.

If only. . .

He gritted his teeth and waited for whatever was going to happen next.

CHAPTER SEVEN

"Cast off," the pirate captain called.

One of the *Henrietta*'s crew let go of the line that had been pulling the *Cockleshell* behind her, and the small craft began to separate from the large one.

Already several of the crewmen had gone below the narrow deck of the *Cockleshell* to begin working the hand pump to eject the water that was pouring rapidly through the seacock the pirates had smashed before they turned the small boat over.

"We were lucky," Raider observed to Captain Mason, who was seated beside him in the narrow confinement of the *Cockleshell*'s cockpit. Being on a small craft like this one, Raider could see, was something quite different from sailing on a ship the size of the *Henrietta*. Yet, oddly, even though there was more motion involved on the small boat, he was experiencing much less in the way of an ailing belly from it. There was not only more motion, it was a different motion, and it didn't seem to bother him so much. This feeling was livelier somehow and less threatening to the senses.

Mason gave him a dark look. "Don't you say that to me, mister. Don't you never say that again. Lucky? Jesus!"

"I meant that everyone is still alive and unhurt," Raider explained to the distraught and now shipless ship's captain.

Mason's answer was a grunt. He turned his face away from Raider and stared toward the mainland shore.

"Cap'n, sir?" McInally asked. "Shall we make for home or beach 'er, sir?" Obviously this was a situation in which the mate could not take charge. They were far beyond the normal now.

Mason barked a question below about the pumping.

"Just about keeping up with it, sir. We can hold 'er if you want."

"Make for port, Mr. McInally," Mason ordered.

"Aye aye, sir." In a sharper voice he added, "Make sail, lads. Mr. Horstfutter, set your pump watches, and mind you change 'em regular, sar. We've only a few hours to home, lads, so stay at it."

Ahead of them the undamaged *Henrietta* was drawing farther away as the weight of the incoming water pulled at the *Cockleshell*.

"Damn you. Damn you t' the deep," someone muttered at the receding stern of the *Henrietta*.

Raider opened his bag and replaced his gunbelt around his waist. Not that the gesture would do much good now, but it made him feel better.

Silently he added his agreement with the sailor who had just spoken.

Damn them anyway.

CHAPTER EIGHT

Jon Harwig was a large man, at least as tall as Raider and outweighing the Pinkerton operative by a good seventy pounds or more. He had the appearance of a man who had been a bull in his prime, but now, in his sixties or thereabouts, the muscle had gone soft, and it would have taken a very good tailor indeed to hide the fact that most of the man's bulk was now flab. Jon Harwig did not have a particularly good tailor.

He greeted Raider with apprehension instead of warmth. "I realize you were inconvenienced, Mr. Raider, and I am sure Captain Mason already expressed our regrets—my regrets personally as well, of course—but if you expect some sort of compensation for your trouble . . . I mean, you *did* arrive safely to Rockport, which is where you were ticketed to go, and . . ."

Raider grinned and introduced himself more fully as an operative working on behalf of the Gulf Insurance Company.

Instead of relief or pleasure, though, Harwig's reaction to the information was to slump into his chair and begin to wring his hands.

"Oh, Lord! Don't tell me. They're dropping me, aren't they? After all these years, they're dumping me now that I need them. Not that, too. I'm . . . I'll be ruined. Ruined! As if things weren't already bad enough. Now I'm ruined altogether. Oh, Lord." The man looked like he was ready to break down.

"Whoa," Raider said. "They sent me here to help you, man. Surely you can understand that. After all, they're the ones who are out for the losses."

Harwig gave him an anguished look. "You think *they* are the ones who are out? What about me? What about all the men who work for me? You think we aren't affected by this? Oh, sure, on paper it looks as though it's the insurors who stand the gaff. But do you think they cover everything? Of course not. I can only carry coverage enough to meet the basic costs of run-down ships. Every loss of a ship involves more than the ship and the cargo. I have to pay the difference out of pocket, sir. Cordage, sails, tools, edibles, water casks, lamps and lamp oils, signal flags—why, the list is endless. Endless. And none of those things are covered by insurance claims. And it is becoming difficult—indeed, almost impossible—for my agents to find cargoes for me to ship. Consignors are demanding proof of insurance from me at outrageous levels already. Why, I believe the few who still use my ships are overclaiming their values and actually *hoping* to see their cargoes lost. It is . . . terrible. Just terrible. It's ruining me, Mr. Raider. It's just ruining me. And now . . ." He was able to stop short of actually sobbing, but he turned his head away from Raider and sat in silence for some time. When he spoke again it was a low moan such as a wounded animal might make. "Why? Why me?"

Raider waited patiently, interested in Harwig's reactions but feeling no particular sympathy for a man who allowed himself to display such a state.

Finally, when Harwig again seemed under control of himself, Raider said, "You ask an interesting question, Mr. Harwig. Why you?"

"Pardon? I mean, what is it you're driving at, man?"

"It's a simple enough question. Why you? Why, specifically, is it *you* that the pirates are picking on? For that matter, *is* it only you that the pirates are raiding? The insurance company only has records on their own clients, you know. So they couldn't tell me if there've been other incidents of piracy along this coast. I don't really know if you're the only target of these pirates or if there are other ships and shipowners who've been hit."

"Why, as a matter of fact, I'm the only one. The only one who's reported any losses to pirates." Harwig made a face. "Not that everyone believes that, mind you. Pirates! Who the hell would believe that in this day and age? Piracy went out of style half a century ago. More, really. I . . . I daresay there are many people, seamen even, who believe we're making this whole thing up. They just don't believe it. Some of them." Harwig sighed. He looked and sounded like a man already beaten by his enemies.

Still, Raider realized, that *could* be an act Harwig was putting on. The man could be as Morton Bell suspected, a fraud and a cheat who was making a fat, last profit from the insurors by arranging for the "pirates" to take his own ships.

The ships's crews would not necessarily have to know that their employer was behind the piracy.

And certainly all reports thus far indicated that the pirates were careful to preserve the lives, even the comforts, of the crew and passengers of the ships that had been taken. There were threats, as Raider had seen for himself. But no one had ever been harmed when a Harwig ship was being taken.

And if some independent crowd of pirates really were operating on the south Texas coast, why the hell would they choose to pick on Jon Harwig and on Jon Harwig alone?

Raider's own limited observations pretty clearly showed that Harwig was neither the biggest nor the richest shipper on this stretch of water. Many—many? hell, most—other ships he had seen at New Orleans, at Galveston, at Port Lavaca, and here in Rockport were larger and finer and better fitted than Harwig's fleet of lumbering old buckets.

So if there truly were pirates, why in hell wouldn't they be taking the richest pickings instead of just this man's?

There were other observations, too, that lent spice to that same question.

For instance, the men who had boarded and stolen the *Henrietta* already knew the ship, knew its movements, asked for its officers *by name,* for crying out loud.

The taking of the *Henrietta* was no random happenstance. The pirates had been lying in wait for precisely that ship and for no other. Raider was sure of that much, anyway.

He knew better than to openly raise his doubts with Harwig, though. The man was already acting as good as whipped. If Raider wanted to get any help from him—whether to hang a pirate or Jon Harwig himself—he was going to have to present a sympathetic front to the aging shipowner.

"What anyone else thinks isn't the point," he said. "The insurance company hired the Pinkerton Agency and sent me here at considerable expense to find out who is responsible for your problems, Mr. Harwig." He smiled. "And to stop those problems."

"Don't get me wrong, Mr. Raider. I am grateful to the company and to you. Any help I can give you, any questions I can answer, anything at all. Just call on me or on any of my men. Anything at all. You have my word on that. Anything."

Raider nodded and leaned forward. "Then I want you to tell me everything you know and everything you suspect. Not just the facts, mind, but every thought you've had about this, no matter how farfetched it sounds." He smiled again. "After all, Mr. Harwig, there may be some folks who doubt that piracy still exists, but I'm not one of them. I've been there. I saw the pirates and I had their guns held on me, so at least you don't have to convince me that the pirates are real."

For the first time since Raider entered Harwig's office there was something like relief in the man's expression.

He began talking and did not stop for a very long while.

CHAPTER NINE

Raider paused outside the unimpressive offices of the Harwig Line and was able to take time now to get a look at the coastal community of Rockport. When the waterlogged *Cockleshell* had got in last night he had only been thinking about finding a room and a drink. Now, in daylight, he saw that Rockport was a gray little town that looked as if it had seen better days. Like Harwig and his ships, Raider thought uncharitably. Town and ships and man alike looked as if they had weathered a few too many storms between refurbishings.

The town was built on the edge of Aransas Bay, inside the protection of San Jose Island from the sometimes stormy waters of the Gulf. It was a sandy, sunbaked, windswept little place.

Once, he had been told, Rockport had been the rising star of Texas's coast. But that was back when much of Texas was overrun with beeves gone wild during the war years when there was no one at home to tend them. Then, after the war, there was no money for anyone to buy them. The wild longhorn beeves of south Texas were worthless except for their hides and tallow.

Even at a time when children in the war-torn East lacked meat in their diets, the Texas steers were worthless because there was no way to transport their meat without spoiling.

Rockport was an outgrowth of that era, and hide and tallow factories sprang up on the sandy coastline to slaughter cattle by the tens of thousands, the hides preserved and sold to be made into leather, their fat rendered into nonperishable tallow, and their bones sold for fertilizer. Only the meat was wasted.

Cattlemen shuddered, but sold all the beeves the tallow factories would take, usually for only a few dollars a head. The factories and the shipowners prospered during those times.

The coming of the rails to Kansas and the opening of new eastern markets still hungry for meat signaled the beginning of the end for Rockport and the few other towns like it.

Now, on a slightly overcast day with the tang of salt-smell in his nostrils, Raider could see more than a dozen of the ungainly, unpainted tallow factories ranged around the outskirts of Rockport.

There was smoke coming from the rendering fires in only three of them, though. Nowadays the cattlemen sold their beeves elsewhere, at far better prices, and only a few aging or misshapen culls were brought to the factories to be sold for the value of their hides.

All the rest of the once proud factories were shut down and falling into ruin.

Even the mountain-sized bone heaps had been cleared away and shipped east to be dried and crushed and used for the manufacture of fertilizers.

Rockport was not, Raider thought, a picture of prosperity.

Even much of the shipping trade had gone elsewhere: south to Corpus Christi, north to Galveston.

Now Rockport had a handful of stores, a handful of homes, three hotels, of which only one remained open for business—and of course its docks, where so many shattered dreams had been shipped out to other, more prosperous ports.

It was a hell of a place for a pirate to choose as his target, Raider thought.

Judging from appearances alone he would have had to guess that the entire population of Rockport couldn't put together enough of a poke to justify a highwayman's trouble for one afternoon of thieving.

Yet it was here that the pirates were hitting.

Not just because it was Harwig ships they were taking either, but because for some reason the pirates chose to take the Harwig ships invariably within close range of Harwig's home port.

That was illogical, Raider thought, but it was nevertheless a fact. And facts were something he had learned not to argue with.

No matter how illogical the pirates' selections seemed to Raider to be, they would actually prove to be entirely, perfectly logical. *To the pirates themselves*. That was the thing. To the men committing the crime, their actions would seem entirely reasonable and right. Probably even necessary.

Raider's problem right now was that he didn't know how or why these crimes should be logical for someone.

If he could work that out, he would probably know as well who was behind the piracy, whether it was Jon Harwig himself or some other party, someone operating for reasons of his own.

Reasons, Raider thought, that should become clear enough in time if he did his part.

He sighed. Which wasn't going to happen if he just stood around on the steps in front of Harwig's building and admired the town.

First he was going to have to go out and *do* something.

And before *that* he was going to go have breakfast. He hadn't taken time for that before he went to meet Harwig, and now it was approaching lunchtime. He was damned well hungry.

He set aside his concerns about the assignment for the moment and headed back toward his hotel.

CHAPTER TEN

There was something to be said for a tallow factory town after all. Beef here was still mostly considered a waste product. Twenty-five cents bought him two eggs, toast, and more broiled tenderloin than three hungry men could put away. That seemed mighty strange until you realized that there isn't any fat in a tenderloin, so the things were useless to the tallow processors. Sure made for good eating, though.

Raider considered, decided he could not possibly hold another mouthful, and reluctantly pushed his plate—plate, hell, the thing was a platter big enough to carry a Christmas goose —away. He reached for his coffee cup.

Although he had just finished his breakfast, the lunch-hour trade was beginning to enter the hotel restaurant, which seemed to be one of the few places remaining in Rockport where you could buy a decent meal. Several restaurants in town had closed down, and one building that still showed a sign reading "Café" high on its false front was now a store selling used clothing and crudely homemade leather goods.

Raider saw a familiar face among the people filtering into the hotel restaurant and motioned for the man to join him.

"Aye?"

"I was going to look you up this afternoon, Mr. McInally. You'd save me the trouble if you would join me for lunch. My treat, seeing as it's in the line of business."

"Huh. I could do with a free meal, Mr. Raider. Seein' as how I'll be outta work now." McInally pulled out a chair opposite Raider and sat down heavily.

"I'm sorry to hear that, Mr. McInally."

"Oh, 'tis only t' be expected. No point replacing the poor old *Henrietta*. What Jon'll get from the insurance comp'ny won't do much toward putting another ship afloat. An' Lord knows the man hasn't enough left to go on much longer nohow. The *Henrietta*'s crew is only out employment by a few months sooner than the rest of the lads will be."

"Really?" That was something Harwig had neglected to mention to Raider. If true, that is. It could be that the former first mate was wrong. Or it could easily be that Jon Harwig didn't want to whine to a stranger about his financial difficulties.

"So it's really of little matter. An' I'm not too proud to let an outfit like the Pinkerton Agency pick up me tab for a meal." The waiter came over and McInally ordered a dinner of broiled tenderloin and all the trimmings. The menu listed the meal at thirty-five cents—nearly all profit, in all probability.

"You heard about that," Raider observed after the waiter was gone.

"Aye. Heard it in the office a bit ago when I was being given the sad news. By now I expect it's all over the docks."

So much for any thoughts about being able to sneak around undercover on this one. Raider hadn't yet planned out just how he intended to tackle the problem of ferreting out Jon Harwig's pirates. Now it looked as if his choices were limited. It was his own fault, though, he conceded. He hadn't thought to ask Harwig to remain quiet about who Raider was and what he was doing here.

And of course if Harwig was really in financially troubled waters, it could well be that the man would want to use Raider's presence as a Pinkerton operative to hold out as a carrot so his creditors would remain silent for the time being.

"Did anyone suggest how my questions should be treated?" Raider asked. If there was any hint that his presence here was to be resented by the seamen it might point a finger back into Harwig's private office. If not, though, it wouldn't necessarily mean that Harwig was innocent. It could only mean that he was bright about stealing from himself.

"Aye," McInally said. "We was all told to help you every way we could. There was some hint—not a promise, y' see, but a hint—that we might have jobs again if you find them pirates in time."

Hoo boy. Not that anyone was applying any pressure about

this one, Raider thought. All Raider was responsible for now was the future health and happiness of Jon Harwig and every one of his employees and their families. Not a comforting thought.

Raider said nothing about that, though. He nodded and said instead, "The reason I wanted to see you was to find out if you've learned who owns the boat that the pirates stole. The *Cockleshell*."

McInally smiled. "Ah, I understand. Good thinkin', Mr. Raider. You want to see if you can get a line on the pirates from where an' when they took the wee craft. Like if someone saw 'em at the thieving or such."

"Yes," Raider said with a weak smile. "Something like that." Now it looked as though not only had the Harwig people been asked to cooperate, they were going to *participate* in the investigation. Saints preserve a man from well-meaning amateurs, Raider mentally cried.

What the hell, though. If he didn't do any good down here, maybe Morton Bell would put in a good word for him and he could take up peddling insurance for a living. If nothing else it would be better-paying work than the Pinkerton Agency offered.

"Good thinkin', Mr. Raider. Very good," McInally exclaimed with satisfaction.

"I'm glad you approve," Raider said dryly.

"An' as a matter o' fact, sar, I did learn whose boat the cunning thing be."

"Mmm?"

"Belongs t' Lucy Barnes," McInally said, a note of finality in his voice that said that should explain everything.

"Lucy Barnes?" Raider inquired. Maybe the name alone explained something to a Rockport resident, but not to a newcomer.

"Oh, you wouldn't be knowing about the widow Barnes, would ye?"

"No," Raider agreed. "I wouldn't."

McInally's dinner arrived, and the man began sawing off great hunks of meat, cutting the tenderloin into huge bites and chewing industriously while he talked.

"Lucy—the widow Barnes, that is—is a local lass who made good. Grew up here. Grew up poor, but that never stopped her. Lovely woman, y' see. Lovely. Half the young men on the coast were mad in love with her when she was a girl." McInally laughed around a mouthful of beef. "Not so many have got over it neither, let me tell ye. But she moved off when she turned of age. Sold the boat her dead daddy had left her an' moved away somewheres. Must've married well, though she never talks of that. Came back just a year or so ago with some money t' put in the bank and bought out the chandlery that'd once been in her mother's family. Lovely woman still." He winked. "But so far no one's been able t' get her to forget her husband, though Lord knows there's been enough young salts as have tried. The young ones are panting after 'er, and us old ones all claim her as one of our own. She's a real credit to her upbringing, y' see. Why, there's never a sailor boy hurt but that Lucy isn't there to offer her own hand to his healing and never a broken-down old has-been that she won't stake till he finds a new berth. Lovely girl." McInally shook his head admiringly and stuffed his mouth with another chunk of beef.

"And you say she's the one who owns the *Cockleshell*," Raider said, trying to return to the business at hand.

"Aye, she does. Loves the water, that girl. An' no wonder. Her daddy was a sailor man. The real thing, not like some of these young pups. Old Bryce, he knew the winds an' the shoals all right. From Kingston t' Cartagena, he did. Old Bryce was no coaster, either. As a boy he'd sailed a whaler out o' Bedford. Came down here hauling cargo for the Army when they put the whupping on the Mexicans an' stayed to let the sun o' this country warm the salt in his beard. Oh, he was a seaman, all right. So the lass gets her love o' the blue water honest enough. She keeps the little boat just for pleasure, I take it. And no wonder it's fast and fitted so nice, her owning the chandlery now. I give her that coin the pirate sent for her repairs an' her troubles. You shoulda seen her laugh when she found where it come from." He shook his head again. "Lovely woman. Not that she's in need of charity from some damned pirate, mind. But she did get a laugh outta that coin." McInally attacked his meal again.

"This chandlery . . . ?"

"You can't miss it. Big place right off the wharf. Best-kept building in town nowadays. Lucy sees to that. You'll likely find her there anytime during business hours. She's bright. Keeps her sails trimmed close t' the wind, that girl." He took a gulp of steaming coffee to wash down some of the meat he had been swallowing and added, "I'd have asked her myself about the theft of the wee boat, but I never thought to."

"No harm done," Raider assured him. "I'd have gone back and talked to her myself anyway, and this way she won't be bothered any more than is necessary."

McInally winked at him. "Just don't be s'prised if you fall in love with her yerself, lad. Nearly everyone does." He laughed and stabbed another chunk of beef.

Raider stood and dropped a coin on the table to pay for both meals.

"Thanks for the dinner, Mr. Pinkerton-man."

"My pleasure, Mr. McInally." The man was still eating and calling for more meat when Raider left.

CHAPTER ELEVEN

Raider could see what McInally meant about the chandlery run by the widow Lucy Barnes. The building occupied half of a city block and faced the wharves of Rockport across a wide avenue where freight wagons serving the ships could have access to land and bay.

The chandlery—whatever the hell *that* was, Raider was a bit hazy about what to expect inside—was two stories tall, with a scalloped, gold-painted false front on top of the whole huge mass of the structure.

Unlike most of the weather-graying buildings of Rockport, the Barnes Chandlery was tidily painted a slate blue color with bright, startlingly white trim. It looked like a building that somehow had been picked up off the New England seacoast and plunked down here on the Texas Gulf. The place was so big that there were several different "front door" entrances along the length of it and a loading dock conveniently placed at the south end. All in all, damned impressive, Raider thought.

He looked it over first and paused to take a look as well at a coastal freighter showing the Harwig Line colors that was tied up across the way from the big building, then went inside.

Raider wasn't sure what he had expected to find in a chandlery, but it turned out to be like a department store, like a *big* department store, with all the departments devoted one way or another to ships and shipping.

An entire section of the store was devoted to rope. More accurately, he suspected, to ropes, cables, lines, hawsers— sailors seemed to have a whole vocabulary devoted just to

45

ropes. Some of them he'd even heard called sheets, which made no sense whatsoever, but they did it anyway.

Next to the ropes there were chains. And lamps. And lanterns. And anchors. And jerseys. And pants. And ducky little caps. And oilskins. And log books. And strange-looking, expensive-looking instruments, the uses of which Raider couldn't begin to guess. And brass doodads that fell into the same category of the unfathomable. And bulk foods. And oil. And oakum. And—acres of the shit, practically.

Whatever a man needed for the rigging or the sailing or the provisioning of a ship, either it was already here for sale or the guy probably didn't need it as bad as he thought he did.

It was just that kind of place.

Of course, what a big outfit like this would be doing in a has-been backwater like Rockport, well, that would have to be a whim of the owner. In New York or Boston or San Francisco or New Orleans, sure. But in Rockport?

It takes all kinds, Raider thought.

An elderly clerk who looked as salty and weather-beaten as a chunk of driftwood came over and gave Raider a good looking over, obviously taking in the tall operative's non-nautical clothing, before he inquired what kind of help the visitor might need.

"I came to see Mrs. Barnes," Raider said politely.

The clerk cocked his head and squinted past bushy eyebrows for a moment. Then he grunted. "You'd be the Pinkerton man then." It wasn't really a question. More like an accusation.

"That's right."

Well, McInally had said the word would be getting around. The man sure hadn't lied about that.

The clerk grunted in a clearly disapproving manner, but he pointed toward a staircase at the back of the huge store area. The stairs led up to a sort of balcony arrangement hung halfway up the back wall in the cavernous interior of the place. A plate-glass window looked down over the store from the office, so anyone in there could keep an eye on the floor below if they so chose.

"Mind you knock before you go in," the clerk warned. "And if Miz Barnes don't want to see you, don't you be pushy or you'll be out on yer ear."

The old boy was half Raider's size and twice Raider's age,

but that discrepancy sure didn't seem to intimidate him any. He sounded like he damn well meant it. Raider found the threat more amusing than worrisome, but he was careful not to let that show.

"Thank you."

"And take yer damn hat off."

"Okay. Thanks." Raider chuckled and removed his black Stetson. Which probably did look wildly out of place here, come to think of it, in spite of Texas's reputation as cow country.

The old clerk finally turned away to go about his business of tidying the stock on some shelves—shelves, Raider noticed, quite near the stairs leading up to Mrs. Barnes's office—and Raider went upstairs and knocked lightly on the frosted glass of the door.

"Come in."

The voice was a woman's, but when Raider stepped inside he was disappointed. After all, McInally had stressed what a beauty Lucy Barnes was and how all the "young salts" were sniffing around behind her. And the old fellow downstairs acted as if he was half in love with his boss too. Yet the woman who sat at the desk facing Raider was middle-aged and, frankly, dowdy. Her hair was done up in a severe bun, and her dress was plain. But in her case there wasn't much of anything artificial that could have been done to improve on the poor pickings nature had given her to start with. Raider decided that the men of Rockport were in a bad way if this was their local siren.

He cleared his throat and bobbed his head in greeting. "My name is Raider, ma'am. Representing the Pinkerton National Detective Agency. I wanted to ask some questions about the disappearance of your boat, the *Cockleshell*."

"You don't want me, then, Mr. Raider. You'll want to speak with Mrs. Barnes. One moment, please, and I'll see if she's free now."

The secretary left her desk and disappeared through a door into another office.

A moment later Raider revised his opinion of the men of Rockport. They weren't daft after all.

CHAPTER TWELVE

Lucy Barnes was okay. If, that is, you approved of tall, statuesque redheads with a figure that would put the Venus de Milo to shame and a face that any sane portrait artist would give his life savings for the privilege of painting.

If that was your sort of woman, well, Lucy Barnes was all right.

The younger men of Rockport panting after this woman? Hell, it was a wonder they weren't tripping over themselves to get at her. They should have been lining up on the quay just to get a glimpse of her.

Raider felt a surge of desire for the extraordinary woman as soon as she came into sight to greet him, and he knew damn good and well it was not going to get any easier. A woman this beautiful you just didn't get used to. This one was . . . special. No wonder the old boy downstairs was so protective of her. No wonder McInally got such a charge out of the young men's reactions to her. Raider strongly suspected, though, that he would never reach an age when a woman like this would fail to stir him. That wasn't being old, it was being dead. If a man's body was still warm he would have to get a hard-on from being in the same room with Lucy Barnes.

She was nearly as tall as Raider, with a poise and carriage that said she was well aware of her beauty. Her eyes were green and her skin translucently pale. Although she was already widowed, he doubted that she had yet seen her thirtieth birthday.

This one, he thought, would be quite a handful. Better yet, quite an armful.

It occurred to him, finally, that he had been standing in the doorway of her office for some time while he absorbed the rather extreme impact of the widow Barnes.

She gave him time, obviously accustomed to this reaction, then smiled a welcome that pretended she was just a simple businesswoman greeting a visitor. "Mr. Raider? I understand you want to see me. I assume that you are the Pinkerton detective investigating the piracy of Mr. Harwig's ships?"

"Uh, yes, ma'am. But we prefer to be called operatives, not detectives, ma'am."

"Very well, Operative Raider. Come inside. I believe we can discuss this more comfortably if we are not standing in the doorway, don't you?" Her smile did interesting things to the shape of full, soft-looking lips. When she turned and went back to a huge desk in the small office area he saw that her walk was as elegant and controlled as her appearance.

Raider hoped his tongue wasn't dangling at any level lower than his kneecaps. After all, a man has his pride. It wouldn't be seemly to step on the thing while he was walking.

Mrs. Barnes—whoever Mr. Barnes had been, he was one lucky son of a bitch, even if he was dead now—motioned Raider into a leather-upholstered armchair and took her own rather more substantial seat with all the grace of a queen taking her throne. Or at least what Raider thought a queen *ought* to look like.

Raider thought about it for a moment and decided he was probably making an ass of himself. The woman was undoubtedly a true beauty, but he was willing to bet that she farted whenever she ate beans just like anybody else. Thinking about that let him get a better handle on the situation. He was here to do a job, and this was somebody he had to talk to while he was trying to get it done. No more than that. Regular old stuff, no matter what this person looked like. Routine.

Sure it was.

He cleared his throat. "I need to ask you about the *Cockleshell,* Mrs. Barnes."

"Yes. I understand my pretty little boat was stolen by the pirates before the, um, most recent incident."

"Yes, ma'am. I happened to be aboard the *Henrietta* when she was taken. The crew and I reached Rockport on your boat last night."

"So Mr. McInally explained to me this morning. But I am

afraid I shan't be of much help to your investigation, sir. You see, I hadn't known the *Cockleshell* was stolen until Mr. McInally came by this morning to tell me it had been returned." She smiled. She was even more lovely when she smiled, damn it. "And to deliver the damage compensation paid by the pirates. Rather odd of them to think of that, don't you agree?"

"Yes, ma'am. You say you hadn't known the boat was missing?"

"No. But then I only have time to use it on weekends. Very rarely otherwise. The *Cockleshell* is really more than one person can comfortably manage. Certainly more than would be pleasant for a solitary sail in the evening. I keep her tied up at my country home. During the week I stay in town, and I have a cat-rigged skiff here that I sometimes take out in the evening. But the *Cockleshell* would be too much trouble for that."

Raider had damned little knowledge about small boats, but he supposed the whole thing would make sense to someone who did.

"Do you sail, Mr. Raider?" Lucy Barnes was giving him a level-eyed gaze that might—or might not—hold a hint of invitation in those green, green eyes.

"No." He smiled. "But I'd sure like to learn."

She looked away, those lovely eyes focusing on some distant, unseen place. "It is delightful, really. Moving with the wind. Floating over clear, perfect water. It is quite as close as a person can come to flight. It always makes me think of how the birds must feel when they soar on the wind."

"Really?"

"Oh, yes. Delightful."

"Perhaps you would teach me sometime."

The smile returned. "Perhaps I would."

It was an intriguing prospect and worth investigating further. But not at the expense of the business at hand. "So you didn't even know the boat was missing until Mr. McInally saw you this morning?"

"That's right. I hadn't seen the boat since I tied her up last Sunday afternoon. I drove into town that evening and haven't been back to the beach house since. Naturally I was distressed to hear that my dear *Cockleshell* was used in the commission of a crime. But when you think about it, no harm was really done. The damage to the seacock has already been repaired, and the boat is in the ways now while the interior of the hull is allowed to dry. It is a very tight hull. Seldom any water, which is the way I like it. I believe in proper maintenance, you understand. I cannot understand or approve of people who let things run down."

Raider was suddenly conscious of what she must think of his scuffed and battered old leather coat.

"As soon as she has been thoroughly gone over to make sure there was no other damage, I shall have her sent down to her home berth again. But other than that I really could not claim to have been harmed by the incident. I wish I could tell you more, but frankly I haven't any knowledge to impart. About the pirates that is. It *is* the piracy that is the object of your interest, isn't it, Mr. Raider?"

"Yes." He smiled. "And other things."

Lucy Barnes laughed. He thought she'd been pretty when she smiled? There was warmth and beauty enough to melt a glacier when she laughed.

That was the good part. The bad part was that he'd gone and run out of reasons to be here. Mrs. Barnes must have realized the same thing, and she was willing to do something about it.

"I'm afraid I am terribly busy today, Mr. Raider. But if you think of anything else I could help with, anything at all, please call again." She hesitated and lowered her eyes demurely. "Or perhaps sometime we might arrange that sailing lesson you asked about."

Raider felt himself puff up a bit. At that precise moment he could not remember for sure if he had actually asked about sailing lessons or if it was more that she had volunteered the idea. Either way, though, it sounded like a helluva good idea.

"That sounds . . . mighty interesting," he said, standing.

"Yes, it does, doesn't it." Lucy Barnes stood and offered her hand. Raider accepted it with a light touch. Somehow. What he really wanted to do was click his heels and bow over it. Or drop down and lick her palm. Or maybe bark at the moon. Something like that. Instead he just shook her hand briefly and turned to get the hell out of there while he could still walk a straight line. The damn woman had an effect on him, there was no denying it.

"I'll call on you again," he said on his way out.

"I shall look forward to it," she said in a throaty voice that could be interpreted as carrying unspoken promises.

Raider practically floated down the stairs into the chandlery and didn't even mind the dirty looks the old clerk gave him on his way outside.

CHAPTER THIRTEEN

The talk with Lucy Barnes had been satisfying, but only on a personal level. The lady had done nothing to help Raider locate the damned pirates.

He had been hoping to be able to do this the easy way: find the pirates and eliminate Jon Harwig's losses by putting them behind bars.

Now it looked like he was back to the idea of trying to figure out who would want to concentrate on ruining an already fading, and possibly failing, shipowner and let that knowledge lead him to the pirates.

Harwig himself still had to be considered the leading suspect in the case. After all, McInally had said this very morning that the *Henrietta* would not be replaced. Harwig's reasoning for that was that the insurance covered only the loss of the ship and that the costs of refitting a replacement ship with sails, instruments, and other equipment would have to be borne out of pocket—money that Harwig claimed not to have.

So the insurance money paid by Gulf presumably would go directly into Jon Harwig's pocket instead of into a ship to replace the *Henrietta*.

So far, Jon Harwig was the only person who seemed to gain anything at all from the loss of his ships.

Could stolen ships be easily sold? That was something Raider did not know. They must be, of course. Otherwise why steal them? But if a pirate could sell them, so could Harwig. Hell, Harwig could do it easily enough. After all, he was the man who held whatever ownership papers there were on the sailing vessels. Which was just one more thing that Raider didn't know about. A ship was one hell of a big piece of property. Surely there would have to be some ownership papers on the things, like a deed to a piece of land. Or would there be? Damned if Raider knew.

He was beginning to wish that he had asked to be assigned to something simple. Like chasing down a gang of train robbers and putting them all in irons. That he could understand. Or any other normal, land-bound criminal. You just go out and find the son of a bitch and then either face him down or shoot him. Simple. But this bullshit!

He sighed.

Thank goodness Lucy Barnes was up there working away in her office—it sweetened the notion of his having to be down here doing this job.

He took one last look at the imposingly tall front of the Barnes Chandlery and walked back up the main street of Rockport.

He had some time on his hands—the whole truth of it was that he had a *lot* of time on his hands, since he didn't know what the hell to look into first—and thought about hiring a horse. But then, on this case he might not have any need for a horse at all. The pirates and their quarry both traveled on the sea, not the land, so he might better arrange to hire a boat. A boat to take him just where, though, he wasn't sure yet.

Strange damn case, he thought. He felt very much out of his element in Rockport, Texas.

As he walked, he thought. And as he neared the business area of the town his stride increased from an aimless amble to a purposeful march forward.

He stopped at the hotel long enough to encode several different messages, went out again to find the telegraph office, and then headed briskly for the waterfront.

Raider was feeling considerably better by then.

After all, why should a bunch of boat-sailing pirates be all that different from a gang of train robbers?

You just find out who the sons of bitches are and then smoke 'em out.

Raider figured to do something very much along those lines.

CHAPTER FOURTEEN

"What'd you say your name was again, sonny?"

"Raider."

"Oh, yes. The Pinkerton man down here to help Jon." The shipping agent smiled and sat back in his swivel chair.

The agent was aging as badly as was his office—a small, poorly ventilated second-story room above a waterfront bar. The man had a few strands of gray hair combed carefully— ludicrously, really—over a balding dome and cigar ash dribbling down the front of his shabby vest. The office looked as if it hadn't been cleaned since the prosperity went away. And that seemed to have been a very long time ago.

"Now what was it you wanted from me, sonny?"

Raider wasn't exactly used to being called sonny, but the agent—the fading sign on the door at the foot of the stairs said he was A. B. Johnston—was certainly old enough to get away with it.

"I wanted to find out who might have access to information about the movement of ships, Mr. Johnston. Ships and cargoes, too. I was hoping you could help me. If you aren't too busy, that is." The last was a matter of politeness. From the looks of things in Johnston's office, the only time the man would be busy was when he was in a hurry to get to the backhouse. Or maybe downstairs to the bar.

Johnston smiled again, obviously understanding exactly what Raider intended by the comment but not minding it at all. If anything he seemed appreciative. "My pleasure, Mr. Raider. I am rarely busy these days, and I enjoy having someone to talk to." He sighed and twined his fingers together, draping his hands and forearms over a belly that was expanding against the restrictions of his vest.

"Now, to answer your questions, son, why, nearly anyone who's curious would be able to learn the whereabouts of nearly any ship at sea. Merchantmen, that is. Different story entirely, of course, with a man-o'-war."

"But merchant shipping is no secret?" Raider asked.

"Can't be," Johnston said. "Think about it. A man comes in here and wants a cargo sent someplace. He asks a broker to find him a bottom and schedule his load. Now, as a broker, I must be able to tell him that the thus-and-such is carrying a cargo of something or other and she's due to call at so-and-so port, then she can pick up his cargo when she stops at thingamabob. I mean, I have to keep track of what ships are where, where they're going, what they're carrying, where they'll discharge it, and therefore when there will be hold space available for whatever my client wants to ship. And not only that, I have to know where the ship will be going next and where it *can* go if this client wants to consign freight to this ship. You understand me?"

"Yes, I think so. How do you keep track of all that?"

"Oh, it isn't so difficult nowadays, what with the telegraph and all. And of course after all this time I pretty much know the ships that're plying the Gulf. Know where they can make port. Where they're likely to. All that. Ships don't operate on regular schedules like, say, a railroad does, you understand. But there are places they generally call and places they generally don't. It's up to me and brokers like me to keep track of ships and cargoes so we can make our commissions by making the arrangements between the ships and the shippers."

"So you and all the other brokers in all the other ports could look in your books and tell me where a given ship is and probably what she's carrying?"

"That's right. Most times I wouldn't even need to look it up. Most times I'd have it pretty much in mind already where you could find a given ship and what she's likely carrying and where she'll call next."

"So there would be no secret to finding a particular ship. Like one of Harwig's, for instance."

"No secret at all. Can't be or it would be too hit-and-miss finding business. A ship is expensive to operate, son. You have to keep them working if you expect to make a profit on them."

"Mmmm." Raider tugged at his chin for a moment. It seemed there would be no problem if a pirate wanted to find a Harwig ship, then. With or without the connivance of the owner, the pirates could simply ask any good cargo broker and find out all they needed to know about the location of their next target.

"I suppose you would have information about new companies and new ships coming into service too, then?" Raider asked. It occurred to him that those stolen Harwig ships had to be someplace. They were doing something. Otherwise there seemed no point in anyone stealing them. He was beginning to wonder if there might be any brand-new shipping lines operating in the Gulf waters courtesy of an unwilling Jon Harwig.

"Of course I would," Johnston said, immediately grasping the intent of Raider's question. "You're wanting to know if the six Harwig ships have turned up in service someplace else recently, under other names an' other ownerships, right?"

Raider smiled. A. B. Johnston might not look like much, but the old boy was no fool.

"Sorry to disappoint you, son, but the only new bottom come into service in the past year is the *Jenny Mumsen*. She's owned by the Dryden brothers over in Apalachicola, and she was built for them. Every broker on the Gulf has known about her since before her keel was laid. Of course there's been some ships sold now and then, but nothing new except that *Jenny Mumsen*. I wish I could help, but . . ." He spread his hands wide, then returned them to his belly.

"It was a thought," Raider said.

"Of course. But a man couldn't get away with that. Not without every broker on the Gulf catching on to him."

"All right, you would know about anyone setting up a line engaged in freight activity. But what about ships engaged in something else? Would it be possible for someone to use the ships for something else?"

"For what, son? There isn't but so much you can do with a ship but put cargo in her holds. There's cargo and there's passengers. Period. And there isn't a single hull on the Gulf that's carrying only passengers now, unless you count those little mail sloops or like that. And brokers know about those, too. A ship has no value except for what she can carry. They aren't like pleasure boats. Too much crew expense to handle one for pleasure, and they're no damn pleasure anyway. Anyone rich enough to want a pleasure boat, or half a dozen of them, would be able to afford a proper yacht anyway. He sure wouldn't bother stealing some wallowing scow of a coastal freighter for his fun."

Raider grunted.

"Don't look so discouraged, son. Us old-timers in the business of salt and sail've already thought these same things. Asked ourselves these same questions. Why? That's the big one, isn't it. Why would anybody want to take a ship he couldn't possibly use? After all, if he can't profit from it, why steal it to begin with? That's what you are wondering now, right?"

"Right," Raider agreed.

Johnston smiled.

"Competitors?" Raider asked.

The broker's smile became a grin. "Ah. That is, of course, the next logical question. Motive, son. Money naturally being the logical motive for most any crime, right?"

"Right," Raider said again with a nod. He was going to have to remember not to discount shabbily dressed old men in the future. Just because they didn't look like much didn't mean they were fools. A man's brain didn't necessarily deteriorate along with his body.

"Well, I got to tell you, I've wondered the same thing myself," Johnston said. "Jon Harwig is a big part of what business I've got left, you see. When Jon goes under, I'll probably have to retire. Either that or move someplace else, and I'm too set in my ways to want to change now. So I've given this matter some thought. Unfortunately, I can't think of anyone in particular who would benefit from Jon being ruined. I mean, there are a lot of ships working the Gulf, son. Jon's line is hardly the biggest, and it surely is not the grandest line operating. If he goes under, everyone else would pick up his trade. But not any one line in particular. And frankly, he carries so little of the overall traffic, percentagewise, that it wouldn't be a spit in a bucket to the rest of them. No help there either that I can see."

Raider grunted again.

"Frustrating, isn't it," Johnston sympathized. "Of course all of us around Rockport, all around the Gulf for that matter, have worried at that same bone. Frankly, we haven't come up with anything. A lot of good men have put their minds to this, you see. Not just Jon and not just me. We have a personal stake in it, of course, but the other shipowners do too. Piracy is not something we take lightly, son. The people who're preying on Jon Harwig today could turn on someone else tomorrow. It's a problem that worries all the owners, not just Jon Harwig."

"You've been taking it seriously," Raider commented. "Why doesn't the Navy? I understand they investigated the losses. They don't seem particularly concerned."

Johnston snorted. "The Navy. Humbug. They haven't had a war to fight in too many years. Their sailors are a bunch of farm boys who think they look pretty in a uniform. At least the ones we get down here. The glamour ports are all on the blue water. Down here we only get the rejects. Besides, I think they've already been told by someone—I won't try and say who, exactly, though I have my ideas on the subject—but I suspect they've been told it's an insurance scam and they needn't bother looking for piracy."

"I take it you don't believe that yourself."

"I know too much about Jon Harwig's business affairs to believe that, son," Johnston said.

"Harwig couldn't be making a profit off these losses?" Raider asked.

Johnston's response was a loudly derisive snort. "Only a man who doesn't know the business of the sea could believe that. Or some shavetail ensign with more gold braid than good brains."

Raider stood. "You've been a big help, Mr. Johnston. Thank you."

"I've been no help at all, and I know it. But if I can be, you can be sure I will be. Anything you want to know, I'll be glad to help all I can."

"Thank you," Raider said again.

He went downstairs and walked out into the brutal sunshine of the Texas coast.

Motive. A. B. Johnston was certainly right about that: there seemed to be none. Yet there had to be. There was no such thing as a crime committed without a motive. At least not this sort of planned, deliberate crime. Something done from insanity, perhaps, but not this. The piracy of Jon Harwig's ships was carefully planned and carefully reasoned. There had to be motive behind the losses. Yet no one, including people who were expert about—what had Johnston called it?—the business of the sea, could figure out where the profit from the crimes lay.

Damned strange, Raider thought.

Still, if a man was not accomplishing anything, sometimes it was possible to shake the trees and see what fell out just by making someone else believe that he was accomplishing something. And that was exactly the object of his visit to A. B. Johnston and the conversations that were yet to come.

It certainly was no secret that there was a Pinkerton operative snooping around the waterfront of Rockport. And if Raider had no idea where to find the pirates, perhaps he could spook the pirates into finding him.

CHAPTER FIFTEEN

By that evening Raider had talked with damn near everyone on the waterfront of Rockport and very nearly everyone who had business dealings with the sea and with the seamen. And that was very nearly everyone in Rockport, Texas.

By nightfall there was no doubt whatsoever that the entire community had to know there was a Pinkerton operative in search of the pirates.

He had started out asking his questions with intensity and purpose, but for the past several hours he had asked less and seemed to be only barely interested in the responses. Several times he had made lightly veiled comments about "confirming" this or "reaffirming" that.

He wanted someone—any damn one, practically—to start believing that he was really learning something from all the useless chatter. It would have been nice if it were so, of course, but that really wouldn't matter if anyone around Rockport began to believe that it was so.

By the end of the day he was tired and mildly grouchy. But satisfied. He decided to have supper at one of the several waterfront saloons instead of going back to the hotel restaurant. He chose the place below A. B. Johnston's office.

The customers in the loud, smoke-filled place were dressed much differently from the men Raider was used to seeing. Jerseys, cotton trousers, and rope-soled shoes—for those who bothered to wear shoes—seemed to be the order of the day here, and there wasn't a wide-brimmed hat to be seen except for Raider's own Stetson. But otherwise the crowd at the bar was familiar enough. Workingmen seeking relaxation after a day on the job. A few homely whores seeking to profit from the workingmen's wages. The thick smoke was the same as would have been found in a cow-trail saloon, as was the sharp, faintly bitter scent of beer and whiskey.

"Ah, the detective," the bartender said when Raider found a gap in the crowd and pushed his way into it. "Doin' any good, are you, mister?"

Raider shrugged but then winked. "It shouldn't be long now," he said.

"And grand news that is, then. D'you hear that, boys? The detective man here says there'll be jobs ag'in soon for you riggin' monkeys."

There was a round of cheers down the length of the bar, and several of the sailors wanted to buy Raider a drink. If he had accepted all the offers made to him he would have been too drunk to navigate the way back to his room.

"Shush now," he said. "It's much too soon for me to make that kind of promise, boys. I shouldn't have said anything. Do me a favor and forget it, eh?"

The sailors responded with winks and grins, but still many of them wanted to buy him drinks.

"What I'd really like," Raider told the bartender, "is something to eat. Could you arrange that?"

"If you don't need fancy."

"Plain will do."

"Then take this drink—on the house, now—an' light at the table over there. I'll have Maria bring a plate out."

Raider thanked the man and carried the offered glass of bar whiskey to the indicated table.

He looked around the noisy, busy room but saw no pirates lurking in the corners. Not that he had expected to, of course. But, damn, it would have been convenient.

Those pirates had to hole up someplace. And that place couldn't be too terribly far from Rockport. All the boardings had taken place within a relatively few sea miles of Jon Harwig's home port. And the men who boarded the *Henrietta* had known the ship's officers by name. The pirates *had* to be based somewhere close by.

Raider himself had seen at least some of the pirates. He would recognize them if he saw them again. While he was waiting for the pirates to rise to the bait he was throwing out, he could just as well pass the time by looking for the men.

He tasted the whiskey. It wasn't particularly good, but at least it was real whiskey, not some alcohol and horse-piss concoction as might be found inland where freighting was difficult, and it spread a mellow ball of warmth through his stomach.

A man with a shaggy beard and with, incredibly, a brass earring dangling from one earlobe, stopped in front of Raider's table. The man was barefoot and salt-tanned. If ever Raider had laid eyes on a man who looked like a pirate, it had to be this man. But for sure this one hadn't been with the party that boarded the *Henrietta*. This man was not one who could have slipped Raider's memory. Not hardly.

The sailor grinned, exposing yellowed stumps where his teeth should have been. "You find them sons bishes, eh Pinkerton man? You fin' 'em an' bring 'em in here. We do the res', eh." The man drunkenly waved a mug to indicate the others in the place. "We fix them sons bishes good. Keelhaul 'em good." He laughed.

"Keelhaul? I've heard the expression, but what the hell is keelhauling?"

The sailor blinked. "You don' know?"

Raider shook his head.

Several of the other seamen gathered nearer. They laughed and explained.

"Jesus," Raider said. These sailors were a bunch of rough bastards if they would really do something like that to another human being.

"They don' drown," another sailor put in. "You pull 'em under the keel fast so they won' drown."

"That wouldn't be no fun," one said. "Be over too quick."

"You pull 'em under so the barnacles slice 'em up good, like draggin' 'em over a thousan' little bitty knives, see. Then you let 'em get a gulp o' air an' pull 'em under again. An' pretty soon the sharks an' the 'cudas get a sniff o' all the blood, an' they come an' get in on't. An' that's when the sonuvabitch really starts screamin' if you don't pull 'im in."

The explanation brought a round of wickedly eager laughter from the seamen.

"Jesus," Raider said again.

On the other hand, if there had ever been any doubt about where the sympathies of the locals lay, this sure would have cleared up the question.

The pirates were not exactly romantic, popular figures among the sailors of Rockport.

These boys were ready to go for blood in just about the most down and dirty way Raider could imagine. Come to think of it, it was a way he would never have been able to imagine on his own. Lordy!

His supper was brought out by a skinny Mexican girl with straggly hair and a harried, overworked expression. It was a stew of some sort, and thank goodness it was in a gravy instead of a tomato sauce. He wasn't entirely sure he could have held down anything red and drippy right then.

"Thanks for the information, boys." He made a mental note, though, that when he did catch up with the pirates—or they caught up with him—he was going to have to get them to competent authority in a big hurry, preferably somebody way the hell and gone away from this bunch. No son of a bitch ought to have to go through a keelhauling, no matter what he'd done.

CHAPTER SIXTEEN

"Psst!"

"Yeah?" Raider swerved to his left and approached a salty-looking sailor who was bent over an impossibly complicated-looking knot that he seemed to be working on just for the hell of it. At least Raider could not see any obvious function to the thing.

"You remember me from last night, mister? I'm Benjamin. I seen you at the Mermaid." The Mermaid was the name of one of the saloons Raider had looked in on last evening.

"Sure, I remember you, Benjamin." It was only partially a lie. Raider recognized the man's face but never would have recalled his name.

"Don't look now, but there's a fella at the little dock over there. In that blue-painted catboat."

There would have been no point in Raider trying to spot whoever Benjamin was talking about. He had absolutely no idea in the world what a catboat might look like. Unless it was a boat designed for the transporting of cats. Weird thought. Blue he could manage, though.

"What about him?" Raider asked.

"Guy's been through here a couple times this past week. Comes in. Ties up. Has a meal an' gets some supplies. Like that. But he ain't local. Claims he's on a vacation, like. Fisherman. Just for the fun o' it, though. He sure ain't commercial. Got no nets, just some fancy poles an' feather lures and such. Suspicious is what I say. Man's got no business here that we know of."

"You think he could be one of the pirates?" Raider asked.

"Aye, could be. Thought you might wanta look 'im over. Y' know?"

"Thanks. Uh, you say it's a blue *cat* boat?"

"Aye. You know. Catboat."

"Matter of fact, Benjamin, I don't know."

"Oh." Benjamin made a face, probably wondering how a man could reach adulthood without knowing what a catboat was. "Catboat's got one mast, see, set well for'ard, 'most up next t' the stem. Carries a single sail. No jib, see. Easy fer one man t' handle an' fast enough, though a cat won't point upwind so good as a sloop."

That made sense. He supposed. Anyway, the boat in question would be a small one, painted blue, with a single mast set well forward. Raider got that much out of the explanation. The rest of it he just wasn't going to worry about.

Raider made a show of yawning and stretching. When he did so he looked off toward the dock where the small craft tied up on the bay side of Rockport's commercial wharf.

The blue boat was there, just as Benjamin had described it. The catboat was eighteen or twenty feet long and had a tarp rigged to provide a makeshift sort of cabin. It was occupied by a small, raggedly dressed, and most inoffensive-looking little man of indeterminate age.

"I see him," Raider said.

"You might wanta check 'im out. Suspicious is what I call 'im," Benjamin said.

"I think I will." Raider smiled. "I wonder if the fellow'd be willing to hire out and give me a sail. If nothing else it would let me look at the coastline close by. I might get some ideas about where the pirates could be hiding."

"The fella ain't all that friendly. Suspicious. Like I said. But he might perk 'is ears to the clink o' some coins," Benjamin allowed. "Worth a try."

"Thanks for the tip," Raider said.

"Don't let 'im know 'twas me pointed you on 'im," Benjamin cautioned.

"I'll be careful not to."

Raider wandered off into the business district. When he came back to the waterfront a half hour later Benjamin was nowhere in sight, but the little man in the blue boat was still loafing in the sunshine. He had a scaling knife in his hands and was busy slicing a hunk of cheese, making his breakfast from cheese and hard crackers.

"Good morning," Raider said.

The little man squinted up at Raider, frowned, and glanced around before he answered. "Yeah?" There was no particular welcome in his voice.

"Pardon me, but I see that you don't look busy this morning. And as it happens, I need to take a tour along the coast for a few miles up and down from here, having to do with some land I'm looking for. I was wondering if I could hire you to take me out for the day. Perhaps for several days. I would pay, of course. If your rates are not too high."

"I came to fish, not to run a damned water taxi."

Raider smiled. "You could fish and make a few dollars at the same time."

The little man grunted and seemed to think it over. "You say you'd pay?"

"That's right."

"Five dollars a day. In advance," the little man said.

"That sounds fair enough." Raider found a half eagle in his pocket and gave the coin to the fisherman in the catboat.

"Climb aboard, mister. But mind you don't make a misstep. I didn't sign on to haul landlubbers out of the damn drink."

"All right."

The little man steadied the boat, which was rocking gently to the tug of waves and tide and breeze, and held it steady while Raider stepped down from the dock.

"Set there in the stern, mister. That's the back of the boat to you. And keep still. I'll get us under way easier if you keep your hands to yourself and don't get in my road."

Raider did as he was told and watched while the agile little fellow hopped from one end of the boat to the other, tugging at this and tying off that and finally raising the boat's single sail, shoving the boom around to catch the breeze, and then bounding back to the tiller, allowing the wind to fill the flapping sail and pull it snug. It all seemed like so much useless confusion, but within moments the wind was driving the light boat through the water with slowly gathering speed, and the little craft was able to maneuver to the rudder.

While he was at it Raider got a better look at his waterborne taxi driver.

The man was small and slightly built. He probably would have had trouble getting a measurement of five-six unless he drew himself up to all the height he could manage, and he looked weather-beaten around the eyes and the back of his neck, although there was a curious pallor beneath his collar and on his now bare forearms.

He had eyes that were so pale it was difficult to tell if they were a washed-out sky blue or a dove's-breast gray. Whatever their color, they were surrounded by wrinkles.

The boatman was hatless now, but there was a line high on his forehead where the sun had not browned him.

He had not shaved in several days, a fact that contributed to his generally disreputable appearance.

He was wearing lightweight cotton trousers that looked like castoffs long ago rejected by a Mexican peon, and his short-sleeved jersey was several sizes too large for him and was worn hanging slack and slovenly outside the waistband of the trousers. He was barefoot, and his toenails needed clipping.

All in all the fellow was unimposing. Raider suspected the only reason he could be taken for a pirate was because he was a stranger to the seamen of Rockport.

The catboat sliced cleanly through the water, and within minutes they were well out into the mouth of Aransas Bay and standing north, with the onshore breeze driving them at a spanking clip.

The feel of the small boat felt oddly pleasant, something Raider had not been in a mood to appreciate on his only other journey on a small sailing craft, when he and the *Henrietta* crew brought the damaged *Cockleshell* home.

Once they were well beyond the hearing and sight of the men at the wharf behind them the little man began to chuckle.

"You ugly son of a bitch," he said, laughing.

He pulled Raider's five-dollar piece out of his pocket and tossed the coin onto the floor—deck?—at Raider's feet.

CHAPTER SEVENTEEN

Raider grinned and leaned forward—carefully; he didn't want to fall overboard out of the narrow catboat—and clasped the little man's hand.

"Henry Thomas Tillman, what the hell are you doing here?"

Tillman chuckled and said, "I was just going to ask you the same thing."

"Working, what else?"

"So am I, Rade. Same old deal."

Raider shook his head and gave the shabby-looking Tillman a look of amused fondness. Henry Thomas Tillman was an acquaintance who had become a friend during a case in the Indian Territory a while back.

Despite his diminutive size and entirely ordinary appearance, Henry Thomas Tillman was a Texas Ranger. And the little man's reputation was such that he was known as the Tall Man.

Raider had heard about the exploits of the Tall Man for years but had never known that the nickname was a double play on words: Tall Man for Tillman—and a play as well on that peculiarly western form of humor in which short becomes tall, big becomes little, and a fellow with a bald pate must almost necessarily be known as Curly.

Tillman was an oddity among the Rangers, and not only because of his size and inoffensive outward appearance. The Rangers were known to be a crowd of men tough enough to handle whatever came their way—which the Tall Man certainly was—and quick on the trigger.

Henry Thomas Tillman was probably as slow on the draw as anyone Raider had ever seen handle a firearm. The little man needed two hands and ten minutes to get his pipsqueak little revolver—necessarily small and of light caliber because of the unusually small size of his hands—into action.

By way of compensation for that handicap, though, Tillman was also undoubtedly the finest marksman with a handgun that Raider had ever personally observed. Better, in fact, than most wildly exaggerated saloon tales. The "meek" little fellow could take his nickel-plated breaktop Smith and Wesson and light match heads at thirty paces with a one-handed hold and no solid rest. Snuffing candles or shattering hand-thrown lumps of clay by the dozen was simply no trick at all for him.

Besides all of which, Raider just plain liked the man.

The two took several minutes to catch up on their doings since they had last met, while Tillman continued to sail his boat north into the waterway inside San Jose and Matagorda islands, then Raider asked, "So tell me, Tall Man, are we working two sides of the same case again?"

"Damned if I know," Tillman said. "Are you looking for pirates?"

"Sure am. It's an insurance company thing for us."

"And it's just another crime against some Texas citizens to us, Pinkerton man."

Raider shook his head. "Shee-oot, I thought you Rangers only took on cases that involved sweat and fast horses."

Tillman laughed. "And I thought you private gunslicks only took on things that involved no sweat and fast women. I'll tell you a truth, though. I asked for this one when I heard about it. Gives me a chance to get out on my boat and get paid for it while I'm having fun."

"I guess you did say something about that once, but I sure never made a connection with this deal."

"Hell, I'd hope not. I'd ruther nobody knew the Ranger service is on this one."

"Well, it's damn sure too late to keep anybody from knowing the Pinkerton Agency is," Raider admitted.

Tillman grinned. "So I already heard on the waterfront. The whole county knows you're on the job."

"So I stay on the surface and you nose around undercover," Raider suggested.

"Sounds good to me."

"What've you learned so far, Henry Thomas?"

"First thing, I'm not going by my real name around here. Anybody asks, my name is Thomas Henry." He chuckled. "Call me Tom."

"I'll try and remember that."

"Second"—he made a face—"I haven't learned very damn much so far. Spent the past week and a half cruising the coast for fifty miles in either direction thinking I might be able to spot the hole-up. I mean, these ol' boys have to be hanging around some damn place, right? All the captures've been fairly close to home port. So they can't be staying too awful far. Wherever it is, though, I can't spot it just by looking. I mean, I've poked into every inlet from South Padre to Freeport."

"No luck, huh?"

"None."

"An' that tears that, I expect. I was figuring to do something of the sort myself," Raider said.

He brought Henry Thomas Tillman up to date on his own activities and the ruse he was trying to pull on the pirates, then shut up for a moment while the little Ranger tacked to a new heading and trimmed his sail to the new wind direction.

"Hell, Henry Thomas, you act almost like you know what you're doing."

"I ought to. Been messing around on the water about as long as I can remember."

"How'd you ever end up a Ranger?"

Tillman shrugged. "That's fun too, I reckon." He glanced up toward the sail and made another minor adjustment to the main sheet. "Look, I haven't been finding a damn thing so far, and there's a chance that our boys will bite on your play an' come after you. What say you stay out in the open, and I'll lay back and play it cozy. If somebody comes for you, all we got to do is grab him and see what falls out when we shake him."

"It occurs to me," Raider said with a smile, "that I'll be the target again while you doze off in the shadows."

"Hey, if there's gonna be any shooting, bub, better at you than me, eh?"

Raider couldn't help but laugh. The Tall Man sounded so damned sincere. Yet Raider knew good and well that Henry

Thomas Tillman had no idea what it meant to be afraid. Of anyone or anything.

"All right, damn you. I'll play target in the spotlight, then, and you snoop."

"Just exactly the way I like it," Henry Thomas Tillman declared.

"I expect now that we've started on this cruise of yours we'll have to stay out the whole day, though. I don't want to show up back in Rockport too soon when I'm supposed to be out looking for pirates in my hired boat today."

Tillman grinned. "Don't worry. I know a dandy little cantina up in San Antonio Bay. We can lay over there and tell some lies over beer and frijoles. Just so you're sober when I get you back."

The boat hit a surge of choppy water and swayed wildly for a moment. Raider grabbed the gunwale for support and retorted, "Sober, hell. Just so you get me back without drowning."

"Aw, there's no danger. I can swim like a porpoise, personally." The little man deliberately turned the catboat broadside to the chop, and Raider yelped, drawing a gleeful smile from the Tall Man at the sight of Raider's knuckles turning white and his face turning slightly green.

"Hang on, Rade. I'll have you on dry land again in two, three hours."

The little boat shuddered and danced on the crest of a wave, and Raider's stomach began to roll.

CHAPTER EIGHTEEN

It was several hours past dark by the time they returned to Rockport. It was a rather good thing, too, that the sail back down the protected waterway took some hours, because the afternoon had been a wet one, and Raider would have been in no shape to work when they started out. Nor, for that matter, would the Tall Man.

By the time Henry Thomas Tillman tied up at the small boat dock, though, both men were feeling better. Raider's return to normalcy was accelerated by his dumping a large quantity of undigested beer overboard shortly after they left the bayside cantina to the north, a fact that he firmly attributed to Tillman's poor boat handling, swearing it had nothing to do with the tequila they knocked back between beers.

"Thanks, Tom," Raider said loudly after the boat was secured and he was once again on firm footing. "I might want to use your boat again." There might have been ears in the night, and neither of them wanted to tip the locals that the Pinkerton operative was not the only person in the neighborhood interested in the whereabouts of the pirates.

"Five dollars if you do," Tillman said in a grumpy tone of voice. "In advance."

"Yeah. Sure. I'll let you know."

By prearrangement, Raider headed for the Mermaid saloon. He would stop there long enough to let Henry Thomas Tillman get into position to cover him in the streets after Raider came back outside. Moving inconspicuously through shadows was something Tillman did exceedingly well.

Besides, Raider's belly was growlingly empty after his

problem aboard the bouncy little boat, and he was looking forward to the free lunch counter at the bar. The hotel restaurant was probably closed for the night by now, so that would be his best bet for a meal.

Thinking about that and secure in the notion that the Tall Man would be covering his backside, Raider was taken completely by surprise by a flash of bright yellow flame from an alley mouth and the sharp roar of a large-caliber revolver.

He felt a streaking, viciously hot lance of pain slice across the back of his right thigh even as he threw himself forward into a shoulder roll, his hand already sweeping the Remington free of its holster.

He had time to think, almost with a sense of pleasure, that his bait was being swallowed, even as he turned to bring his wrist and forearm on line with the place he had seen the muzzle flash.

The hidden gunman fired again, the slug from the hastily aimed gun striking the ground somewhere to Raider's left and whining off toward the water with a quick, snapping, bee-drone sound.

Raider's big Remington spat in answer, held just to the right of the gun flash.

He heard a solid thump as his slug found hard wood rather than soft flesh, then a scramble of running footsteps as the ambusher retreated at a dead run back through the alley where the son of a bitch had been hiding.

Raider fired again, sending an unaimed shot in the general direction of the pounding footsteps, then tried to jump forward in pursuit.

He tried to and would have, except that his damned right leg was not working particularly well at the moment.

"Damn!" he shouted toward the fleeing assassin. "Damn you!"

Raider shot at the bastard again, but he knew even before he did so that there was no chance at all that he would hit anything.

"Damn you."

He sat back down on the packed sand and crushed shell of the street and felt the back of his thigh gingerly. His hand came away sticky with blood.

A few dozen yards away at the open doors of the Mermaid he could see a few cautious eyes peering out into the darkness.

"It's all right to come out now," Raider called to them. "The guy's gone. And would you bring a lantern and maybe a bit of rope I could use for a tourniquet? I seem t' be doing some bleeding here, an' I'd just as soon not keep it up much longer."

There was a gabble of noise that would have been voices —funny how far away the voices sounded, particularly knowing how close by the people were—and the next thing Raider knew, so sudden that there surely hadn't been time for anybody to walk from the saloon to where he was lying, there were people bending over him with lanterns and some of them still holding drinks in their hands and all of them seemed to be talking at once.

Raider thought it quite funny that they'd gotten there so sudden-like. Really funny. He considered laughing about it, decided to, then found himself blinking and shivering instead.

Damn, but it had gotten cold all of a sudden. Just like that. Cold as a blue damn norther and no warning of the change of weather at all.

Everybody was still talking to him, but the voices all seemed to kind of mix together into a confused drone so that he couldn't pick out any one voice and stay with it long enough to make out what was being said.

Couldn't see so damn well either for some reason. Everything seemed fuzzy around the edges and kind of far away. Even things that looked close enough to touch looked far away.

Raider thought that was absolutely hilarious. He tried to laugh again and this time was pretty sure he could hear himself doing it. Or maybe it was somebody else laughing. He wasn't sure. Wasn't important, anyway. Somebody was laughing. He thought that was pretty nice. Yeah. That was nice.

Sleep would be nice too. He decided he would just close his eyes and rest a bit. He was sure things would look and sound normal again if he could just get a little bit of sleep.

A nap. That was all he needed.

Just a little bit of a nap.

He sighed some and smiled as he let his eyes droop closed.

Oh, it felt awfully, awfully nice to just lay back and let himself float.

Float? How the hell could he be floating? He was on dry

ground, wasn't he? That damn fella with the boat had brought him back to dry ground, hadn't he? Raider was pretty sure that he had.

Still, the floating felt nice.

And he wasn't so terribly cold anymore. Or was he? Didn't matter. He was too sleepy to care just now.

He could worry about that later.

He yawned and smiled.

He would sleep just a bit now. Everything would be better when he woke up.

"Lordy," someone very far away seemed to be saying—or perhaps he was only dreaming that someone was saying that. "I never seen s' damn much blood so quick. Tie 'is leg off. Yeah. Hard, there. An' hurry. Guy's gonna bleed t' death fast if you cain't get that stopped, Charlie."

CHAPTER NINETEEN

Raider's nostrils twitched. He could smell something. Something from very long ago yet hauntingly familiar. Something warm and . . . comforting somehow.

I'll be damned, he thought. Chicken soup.

He opened his eyes, struggling for a moment to release them from the glue of a deep sleep.

He was in a bedroom, but it was not his hotel room nor any room he had ever seen before. He was sure of that.

White chintz curtains billowed softly at an open window, and the wall in front of him held a number of amateurishly done paintings with bold colors and good detail but with the perspectives skewed and sometimes flat. Most of the paintings were still lifes of seashells or net floats or things like that. No, he had definitely never been in this room before.

It took him a while to figure out why he might be here now. Then his leg began to throb, and the memories flooded back.

But all of that had been at night and in the dirt of the street, for sure not in broad daylight in a pleasant bedroom with curtains at the windows and needlepoint-covered throw pillows piled on both sides of him.

So where the hell was he, and what was he doing here?

He tried to sit up, thinking he would go and find out, and discovered that he simply hadn't the energy to do that.

There was not very much pain when he tried to move. He just felt too damn limp to accomplish anything. He felt about as crisp and strong as a leaf of old lettuce. Raising his hand to scratch the itchy beard stubble on his chin was an effort.

Raider blinked and tried to work this out, feeling of his chin again as he did so. If he had this much beard grown, he must have been here several days. Although that made no sense.

Or did it. Lordy, but he was hungry. That chicken soup smell that brought him awake was getting better and better all the time. And making him all the more hungry.

From somewhere down a hallway he could hear someone moving around now, and then some softly spoken words in Spanish. There seemed to be two voices, both female. None of this was making much sense.

He tried once again to get up, or at least to haul himself into a sitting position, but it was no good. He was no more successful this time than he had been before.

With a groan that was more frustration than pain he settled back against the pillows that were propped behind him and closed his eyes again.

The sound of light footsteps pulled his eyes open again. The footsteps were approaching the unfamiliar bedroom.

Raider swallowed hard and had to try twice before he could force any sound through his dry throat. "Ma'am."

Lucy Barnes smiled down at him from the doorway. He had forgotten how pretty she was. Right now she looked like a regular angel with a halo of red hair around that smile. She was carrying a silver tray. Beautiful as Mrs. Barnes was, right at this moment Raider was more interested in the soup bowl she had on the tray.

"You're awake. Good. I was becoming worried about you."

"How . . . ?" There was so much he wanted to ask that he wasn't sure where to begin.

She smiled and shushed him. "Let's get some soup into you first. I'll talk while you eat. Okay?"

He nodded.

She crossed the room with a slow, graceful stride and perched lightly on the edge of the bed beside him.

Having this lovely woman so near made Raider rethink his priorities. Maybe the soup could wait a bit after all.

If she noticed his interest, though, she pretended not to. She pulled back an embroidered linen towel that had been draped over the tray and revealed a steaming bowl of the wonderful-smelling soup, a small plate of dry toast, and a cup of pale, hot beverage that could only be tea. Raider's mouth began to water.

Lucy plumped the pillows behind Raider's neck, then laid the tray across his lap. She picked up an ornate silver spoon and held it to his lips for him.

"Ah." The chicken soup tasted even better than it smelled. He could feel the warmth of it spreading deep inside his belly from the very first sip. "Thank you," he whispered in a husky croak of a voice between sips.

"Good? I'm glad. You need to get your strength back. You lost an awful lot of blood."

"I did?"

"Gracious, we thought for a while we would lose you."

"Where . . . ?" He hadn't time to finish the question. She was already tilting another spoonful of the marvelous soup into his lips.

"You are at my home. My town home, that is. It is quite near to where you were shot, and we certainly couldn't just shove you into a hotel room without anyone to watch over you. My housekeeper—her name is Conchita, and you shall meet her later—has been watching over you while I've been at work."

"But how . . . ?" The ever ready spoon was there to cut it short again. Not that he was complaining, though.

"I happened to be working late that night. The store is only in the next block, you know. Naturally I heard the gunshots, like everyone else in town. And since we haven't a regular doctor of our own, I had them bring you here." Her smile was incredibly lovely.

Raider reached down and touched his thigh. "What . . . ?" There was that damned spoon again.

She smiled and concentrated on feeding him, her own mouth formed into a quite lovely circle as if she were willing him to respond. Finally she answered, "The wound?"

He nodded his head and swallowed.

"As I told you, we have no regular doctor here, but our barber went to barber-surgeon's school back east somewhere. It was a surface gash. Quite clean, he said. The real problem was all the blood you were losing. Once he got that stopped he cleaned the wound and sewed it up. He will come by in a week or so to remove the stitches. And of course since then Conchita and I have been keeping the area clean and watching for infection. It seems to be healing nicely, although I expect you shall have another scar to join all those others." Her smile did not change at all when she said that.

Raider felt his face grow a bit warm, though. He had some other scars, sure, but they weren't all concentrated right in that neighborhood.

It occurred to him suddenly that he didn't seem to be wearing anything under the sheet that covered him now, and he could see his clothing—everything cleaned and pressed and neatly folded—on top of a bureau against a side wall.

Lucy Barnes saw the reaction and laughed. She didn't seem at all embarrassed or disconcerted, though.

Interested, perhaps? He couldn't tell. Certainly there was nothing of the coquette in her manner right now.

She put the soup spoon down for a moment and held a triangle of toast for him to nibble. Damned fancy groceries in the Barnes household, he noticed. The crust of the bread had been neatly trimmed away and the toast cut into tidy wedges. A stray thought flitted through. Why the hell did they call it upper crust when the upper crust didn't eat crusts?

"This is wonderful," he said quite truthfully. "I'm feeling better already."

"Good. The barber said you should recover quickly. Or not at all." She smiled again. "But then, you are in wonderful shape, aren't you."

Again he could not quite decide if there was invitation hidden underneath the words or not.

Even with the growing strength the nourishment was giving him, though, this was no time to fret about it. He doubted he was strong enough to keep a hard-on right this minute, much less do anything with one. Lordy, but he did feel weak.

Better, though. A hell of a lot better than he had when he woke up.

"I don't suppose anyone saw who shot me," he said.

Lucy shook her head, a slanting shaft of sunlight from the window catching the movement of her hair and turning it to red gold. "No. I, we, were hoping you knew who it was. By the time I got to you, of course, half the town was gathered around you." She laughed. "It isn't funny, of course, since it could have been so serious—but fortunately wasn't—but half of them were arguing about what ought to be done, and most of the rest of them were just standing there staring."

"Did you . . . ?"

She shrugged. "One of the men, I don't remember who, already had some rope tied around your leg. I sent someone to fetch Ralph."

"Ralph?"

"Ralph Meyers. He is the barber who sewed you up."

"I see. Then you had me brought here."

"That's right." She fed him another bite of toast and picked up the spoon again.

"I owe you a lot, lady."

"Not at all." The gratitude appeared to make her uncomfortable, so he did not repeat it. But he couldn't help but think that he probably owed this beautiful woman his life.

The ambusher had not had particularly good aim, but the son of a bitch had been lucky enough to make up for that.

For the first time since he wakened, Raider wondered what had become of Henry Thomas Tillman.

They had planned for the Tall Man to pick him up and begin covering him after Raider had had time to stop in the Mermaid and have a few drinks, delaying just to make sure no one noticed the "vacationing" stranger showing any interest in the Pinkerton operative.

The idea of it all had been just fine. But they should have checked with the pirates to make sure they were on the same schedule. Pity the ambusher hadn't waited just a half hour or so to make his move. If he had, the Tall Man would have had him. Damn it.

Raider's eyes drooped closed.

Almost without his being aware of it, Lucy Barnes removed the tray from his lap and slipped out of the bedroom.

Raider quit worrying about Henry Thomas Tillman and let healing sleep reclaim him.

CHAPTER TWENTY

Raider tried to come up behind her without Lucy knowing he was there—he enjoyed watching her work, enjoyed the beauty of her—but she must have heard the tapping of his cane on the quarry tile flooring in the sunroom. She stopped what she was doing and turned to give him a quick, welcoming smile.

"You look chipper today."

"Better all the time," he assured her.

"Good. Now sit over there and be quiet for a moment. I just about . . . have this . . . there!" She daubed a line here, another there, and an impression of a seagull appeared on the canvas she was painting.

Lucy was the artist—in truth only a fair artist, although Raider would never have said so either to or about her—who had done all the paintings in Raider's bedroom and in every other part of the house. The walls were damn near full. If she couldn't work with professional skill she could at least work with diligence, obviously believing that the skill would come in time if only she contributed enough persistence to her efforts.

"Nice," he said.

"I thought I told you to be quiet, sir."

"Sorry," he lied.

He moved his chair a few feet closer to the easel and to a better angle from which to watch her. She was a study in sheer intensity of effort when she was painting, and the northern light in the sunroom—he supposed it really should be called a studio, not because of its use but because it was built on the wrong side of the house to be a sunroom—was especially kind to her.

When she bent to her canvas with a camel-hair brush poised in her hand, she often stuck the pink tip of her tongue out just a fraction of an inch. Raider found the effect of her concentration funny and pretty and touching all at the same time.

"There!" she exclaimed after several minutes. She turned to him and bowed with a flourish. "You may now tell me how very good I am, sir."

"You, ma'am, are very good indeed," he said seriously. He was not looking at her painting when he said it.

Lucy blushed and looked away, staring out through the full wall of glass windows toward the harbor and the town of Rockport.

Raider had been in her home more than a week now—three days unconscious, but the last five recuperating from the gunshot. By now there was only a deep, lingering soreness at the back of his leg, and his strength was returning fairly well. Ralph Meyers said the stitches could be removed in another day or two.

Last night Lucy had come to Raider's bed during the night. Today she seemed shy with him. He hoped she was not regretting the impulse that had brought her to him. Even more, he hoped she would be willing to repeat the visit. She was even lovelier to lie beside than to look at.

"Are you . . . ?" he began, then stopped.

"What?"

He shook his head. "Nothing." Better, perhaps, to not discuss it. There was much about this beautiful and wealthy young woman that he did not understand. But what he did understand, he liked very much.

Lucy smiled and dropped her brushes into an elegant cut-glass tumbler of turpentine for Conchita to clean later. "Are you up to a carriage ride tomorrow?"

"Sure. I can get around fine now. In fact, I was wanting to talk with you about that. It's probably time I move back over to the hotel."

"No!" she said, perhaps a shade too quickly and a shade too loudly. "I mean . . . I would rather you didn't. Those stitches still have to come out, and you might not be comfortable after they are removed. I mean, you could still need some help. Or..." She sighed. In a soft, almost pleading tone of voice she said, "I was hoping you would come with me to the beach house tomorrow. It's Saturday, and I intend to take the whole day off. I shan't even think about business until we come back Sunday night." She blushed, which pleased Raider quite as much as the invitation did. Whatever shyness she was feeling after last night, she wanted to repeat the visit.

"I'm still a little shaky," he said.

"Good." Her voice was very small, and she wasn't looking at him now.

"You've mentioned your beach house before. Is it far?"

"Not terribly. An hour's drive. It isn't really very grand, though. I hope you won't be uncomfortable."

Raider laughed. He doubted that Mrs. Lucille Barnes would believe some of the places he had had to spend his nights in the past. Hell, some of those places weren't even places. Just somewhere to spread a horse blanket and huddle for the night. "Whatever it's like," he said, "it will be fine as long as you're there." Damned if he didn't discover that he meant that too. This Lucy Barnes was getting to him. In a bigger way than he himself had realized.

She smiled again. "How gallant of you, sir."

He grinned. "Is that good?"

Lucy laughed. Whatever the tension or uncertainty she had just been experiencing, it was gone now, and she seemed relaxed and eager for their outing to the beach house.

"It's a wonderful place, Raider dear." He felt a tingle of pleasure. She had never, not even last night, called him "dear" before. "At least for me it is," she went on, not noticing. "I have wonderful memories of the beach house. From my childhood. It was my family's home once. My mother lost it after Daddy . . . died. Then of course we moved away. When I came back that was one of the first things I wanted to do—to buy the old beach house back again. And I did, and I've fixed it up some, but I haven't added to it. I tried to put it back the way I remember it being, but I didn't want to add wings or anything. So it isn't nearly as large or as fine as this house. But I love it anyway."

"I'm sure I will too then," Raider said and meant it.

"Oh, I do hope so." She took the canvas, now a seashore scene with a sandy, curving beach and dunes and sea oats and whitecapped waves in unnaturally blue water, off the easel and set it against the wall to dry.

"Is there anything I can help you with?" Raider offered.

She shook her head, then smiled and said, "You could rest up." Her voice dropped to a whisper. "For later."

Raider laughed. He couldn't remember having been so happy before. Not in a very long time anyway. And certainly not when he had so little to be happy about, at least as far as his work was concerned. He had been inside this house for eight days now and hadn't accomplished a damn thing for Jon Harwig in all that time.

A guilty conscience over that gnawed at him, and he said, "If we're going down to the beach house tomorrow, I'd better let Harwig know where I'll be. Just in case something happens."

"Don't try to walk all that way yourself, dear. I'll send word this afternoon."

"I don't want to be a bother to you."

"Heavens, dear, it's no bother. His people are always in the store for one thing or another. I shall simply have Wallace send up the first Harwig employee who comes in this afternoon and send your message through him. It won't be any bother at all."

"If you say so. Thanks."

She smiled and came to him, rising on tiptoes to deliver a soft and lingering kiss. She smelled and felt and tasted as wonderful as she looked.

He touched her, but she pulled away from him with a show of reluctance. "I really must go back to the store this afternoon. I always take too long with my lunch hours when I get to painting as it is. It would be scandalous if I didn't show up at all. Someone might think . . . might think I was doing what I would like to do but can't today. Do you mind?"

He grinned at her. "Of course I mind, woman. But I understand. Just don't work too late tonight, you hear?"

"I promise." She lowered her eyes and smiled shyly. "I think I may be very tired this evening. I just may want to go to bed early tonight and get a nice *long* sleep before we drive down to the beach house tomorrow."

"Sounds sensible t' me, ma'am."

She laughed, gave him a brief kiss of parting, and was gone.

CHAPTER TWENTY-ONE

After the grandeur of Lucy Barnes's town home, Raider expected the beach place to be something rather special too, all her protestations and apologies aside.

It was, in fact, little better than a huge, sprawling, two-story shed that had been crudely partitioned into separate rooms and floors. Otherwise it would have seemed much like a large and not particularly fine barn, suitable for housing stock of decidedly ordinary quality and bloodline.

There wasn't even a well at the property—something to do with saltwater intrusion. Water for household use had to be delivered and stored in barrels, which were kept in a niche dug beneath the kitchen lean-to and brought into the house by way of a small, self-priming hand pump.

The pump, Lucy explained with some pride, was an innovation she had permitted herself. The old pump had had to be primed and often needed repacking. Except for that, though, the beach house was very much the same as she remembered from her childhood.

Raider could believe that. Fancy it was not.

Lucy hadn't even painted the gray and weathered board-and-batten exterior, preferring to treat the old wood with some sort of colorless varnish to protect it without "improving" it.

Given what she had to work with, though, Raider had to admit that the place was in remarkably good shape. Not a board loose. Not a nail that needed to be driven home.

The site of the old house was a matter of sheer seaside beauty. When they first drove up the sandy path leading to it, Raider had an odd, slightly unsettling impression of déjà vu.

As if he had been here before, seen all this before: the tall, gray, weathered house itself, the dock and small boathouse beyond it, the breezy, windswept curve of coastline with, off-shore, the low dunes of San Jose Island.

That impression was unnerving, because this was the first time he had ventured down the coast below Rockport, either on water or land.

Then he realized that this setting, shown from various viewpoints and in many moods of weather, figured promi-nently in many of the paintings Lucy had made and which hung on practically all the walls of her elegant town home.

He told her about his strange initial reaction to her special place, and Lucy laughed, twining her arm in his and hugging his elbow to her. "Now that you mention it, dear, I suppose I do keep coming back to this happy place in my thoughts and my diversions as well as on my weekends." She smiled at him. Lordy, but she was pretty when she smiled. "This is where my roots are, dear. This is where I belong."

"Then I'm sure I'll like it every bit as much as you do," he said with an attempt at gallantry.

"Good." She hugged his arm again, then concentrated on guiding the light carriage—really more a fancy buggy than an actual carriage—close to the porch so Raider wouldn't have far to walk.

Lucy seemed insistent on the idea that Raider was still an invalid, though his wound had very nearly healed. She was solicitous of him, including in bed, making sure that any walking or other vigorous activity fell to her.

Raider was actually feeling pretty damn good by now, but quite frankly he was enjoying the lady's attentions and had not yet admitted to her just how fine he did feel.

"Shouldn't I help with the horse? Put the rig in the shed? Something useful?" he asked.

"No, Estevan will take care of that. He and his wife look after the place when I'm not here and look after me when I am here. They only live a mile or so inland. If Estevan isn't here already, he will be soon. So you needn't think about anything except enjoying yourself this weekend." Her smile got even wider. "And I shan't have to think about anything except en-joying you, dear."

Raider had had worse offers. There seemed to be no close neighbors, and certainly there was no one else in view. He leaned over and gave her a long kiss, enjoying the knowledge that her breathing quickened every bit as rapidly as his did at the contact.

"I think"—her eyes were wide—"I think we should get inside, dear. Right now. And . . . I shall show you to the bedroom."

Raider grinned and helped her down from the carriage, leaving the horse to stand untended but patient while he hurried inside the rambling house.

After a lunch prepared by a stout, silent, dark-skinned woman who he supposed was Estevan's wife, they carried glasses of cool fruit punch onto the wide covered porch that spread along the full width of the house facing the water. A fresh onshore breeze ruffled Lucy's hair and felt good against Raider's face.

He could see the familiar form of the *Cockleshell* bobbing against its cork fenders at the dockside. Gulls and terns and sandpipers wheeled and dived at the edge of the sand. It was a helluva fine view, and he told her so.

"I love it," she said with a simple but deep intensity.

"So I see." He brought his eyes in from the far blue horizon to the east and looked at her boat. "Hard to believe this lovely spot has been visited by pirates."

Lucy's eyes grew wide and suddenly serious. "What?"

Raider smiled. "I didn't mean to alarm you, dear. I just meant, you know, when someone came and took your boat."

"Oh. Yes." She seemed to relax. "I had actually forgotten. That's terrible of me, isn't it?"

"Not at all." He shifted his glass of punch to his other hand and reached over to clasp her hand in his.

"When you get to feeling better, dear, I must give you that sailing lesson I promised."

"You did?"

"Of course." She laughed. "I remember it quite well, you see, even if you don't." Her eyelids fluttered. "Obviously, you made more of an impression on me at that first meeting than I did on you."

"What?" Then he remembered. "Of course. In your office that first time I ever saw you. You did say something then about teaching me to sail. I'll take you up on it too." The truth was that he felt perfectly capable of going for a sail or a horseback ride or any other damn thing. But he didn't particularly want to admit that to Lucy just yet. "As for what I thought of you that day, ma'am, I expect I'd be willing to go upstairs for a, uh, nap. An' show you just how I feel."

Lucy laughed with obvious pleasure. "Now you are bragging, sir."

"Yes, ma'am. Absolutely. Except that it's no brag if it's true."

"You can't possibly be *up to* it again, dear. Not after this morning."

"Care to make a wager on that?"

She got an impish look about her. "And what stakes do you propose, sir?"

He thought about that some. Then grinned. When he named the wager Lucy first blushed, then threw her head back and laughed loud and long.

"Well?"

"I accept." She set her glass down on the porch floor and stood. "First one upstairs wins the first round." She was off with a swish of flying skirts.

Raider took his time about following. He suspected he was going to need his strength for more important things if he expected to win this particular contest.

On the other hand, win or lose, this was one they would both win.

CHAPTER TWENTY-TWO

Lucy seemed disappointed on Sunday night, after they returned to town, when Raider insisted on going back to the hotel room that had been held for him while he was healing under the widow's excellent care.

"Really, I do have work to do, you know."

She frowned and pouted. "I don't know why you can't stay on with me."

"Now you're being silly. Or at least unrealistic. Of course you know why I can't do that. It's one thing for you to take in someone who's hurt and needs help. It's quite another for you to have a man living with you who isn't your husband." He reached over and squeezed her hand. "The people here love you. They feel protective toward you and proud of you and . . . I don't know what all else. I wouldn't do anything to change that wonderfully high opinion they have of you." He smiled. "After all, ma'am, I have a rather high opinion of you myself."

"Oh, all right. If you must. But you must come see me often." She increased the pressure on his hand. "At night, I mean. And you must promise to tell me everything that you've seen and done and said, just every moment you are away from me. I want to . . ." She lowered her eyes and blushed slightly. "I want to be a part of every moment, you see."

Raider was not sure he could keep from floating right up off the seat of the carriage. Damn! A woman like Lucy Barnes. Flipped over *him*. Absolutely flipped over him. Damn!

He puffed his chest out and grinned and would have leaned over and kissed her right there, except the carriage had stopped in front of the hotel and he didn't want to subject her to a public spectacle like that. But Lordy, he was feeling fine. "Every sight, every word, every thought," he promised. He winked at her. "Every night."

She seemed satisfied with the promise and hugged his arm to her before she let him dismount from the buggy and carry his bag inside.

Raider felt a pang of regret as she drove away toward her elegant town home. This would be the first time in some days that he had to go to sleep without Lucy at his side. He was already missing her.

The sense of loss evaporated, though, when he crossed the hotel lobby and noticed a small, shabby little man busy sweeping the floor of the hotel restaurant and emptying cuspidors.

It was all Raider could do to keep from grinning at Henry Thomas Tillman and giving the Tall Man a wink.

Raider carried his things upstairs to his room and settled into an armchair with the door closed but not locked. He suspected he would be having a visitor soon.

Sure enough, within an hour the door was opened without a knock, and the innocuous little Ranger slipped inside.

Raider grinned at him. "I see you've taken up a new line of work. Something better suited to your talents, is it?"

Tillman made a face and flopped full length onto Raider's bed with a weary sigh. "Hell, Rade, one of us has to try and get some work done around here. All you seem t' be good for is lazing around an' loving up the ladies."

"Why you little son of a bitch," Raider said good-naturedly. "You've been peeking."

"Only some of the time," Tillman said with a grin. "I don't want to get to missing the missus too much, y' know. Us married fellas don't have it so free and easy as you footloose young bucks."

Raider chuckled at the thought of Henry Thomas's discomfort, then became more serious. "Have you done any good?"

The Tall Man frowned and sat up on the edge of the bed. "Nothing to brag about, that's for sure. What I've been trying to figure out is: Why Jon Harwig? I mean, why this Harwig fella in *particular?* You see what I mean? Harwig ships are the only ones these pirates hit. And Lord knows, there's better pickings in the Gulf than his boats. Even calling here at Rockport, there's richer pickings than Harwig has to offer. Or just down the coast at Corpus, there's a world o' shipping traffic comes in and out all the damn time. Ten times the tonnage that Rockport'll ever see again moves in an' out of Corpus. Yet there's never been a ship taken down that way except that one Harwig vessel that was supposed to stop there and then come on home."

Raider nodded. The same question had been plaguing him right from the start of this case. Jon Harwig was an established shipper, but he was far from being the biggest or the best on the Gulf. Yet the pirates hit only ships carrying the Harwig flag. There had to be a reason for that, a reason that probably would be a key to the identity of the pirates.

"What've you found?" he asked.

Henry Thomas Tillman shrugged. "Not a hell of a lot, let me tell you. Of course I can't be asking too many direct questions and callling attention to myself when I'm supposed to be a bummer. But I listen pretty good and, hell, nobody ever sees a guy with a broom in his hand. It's about as close as you can get to being invisible. Which reminds me, I was supposed to be bein' invisible behind your back the night you got shot. Sorry I let it happen."

"Hell, Henry Thomas, you weren't supposed to be in position for another half hour yet. B'sides, I'm supposed to be a big boy now. Big enough to take care of myself without some pipsqueak Texas Ranger to hold my hand. It was my fault, not yours."

"That makes me feel better. Now if you get your thick head blown off some dark night I'll be able to say it was all your fault anyhow. Anyway, getting back to all the things I haven't learned while you've been playing footsie with your nurse, you can ask anybody in Rockport and learn that Jon Harwig is a saint."

"An' I went and missed noticing his halo when I talked to him. You'd think a fellow would spot something like that."

"Seriously," Henry Thomas went on, "this Harwig is a real local hero. You're likely too dense to have noticed it, but ol' Rockport has seen better days. The town isn't dying, quite, but it's damn sure on the downhill slide from the good old days when all the hide and tallow factories were providing employment on the ground and filling ships as fast as they could get in and out again. Those were the gravy days hereabouts. Then the Kansas beef markets opened, and all of a sudden there wasn't a hide and tallow market any more. It's all been downhill since. And the slack's been pretty much taken up by Jon Harwig and his ships.

"He's kept the seamen employed, those that were established here and didn't want to leave, and he's kept some cargoes moving through here that really should've gone through Port Lavaca or Corpus Cristi and likely would have except that Harwig made his rates so damn competitive, and cut his own profits so close, that the owners of the goods could make out better by shipping through Rockport even when their land haulage rates would've been lower through one of the bigger ports.

"And whenever there's been some civic project that needed funding, Harwig has been the first man in line to pitch in with cash or workmen on his payroll or whatever else has been needed. Like I said, the man's a damn saint to hear the townspeople talk about him."

Raider grunted. This kind of information sure as shit wasn't going to point fingers at any suspects.

"There could be something more interesting in Harwig's background," Henry Thomas said. "Though I don't have any hard information about that. I mean, it isn't anything that people would be talking about *now*. You see? And I've been eavesdropping but not asking any open questions. That's the sort of thing you can do better than me, since you're out in the open on this one. I've just picked up . . . oh, I don't know that you'd even call it a hint, more like an impression that maybe Harwig wasn't always thought of as the saint of Rockport. So maybe there's something from way back that would give us a clue."

"I'll find out," Raider said. "As you say, it's the sort of thing I can get into where you couldn't."

The Tall Man nodded. "Meanwhile, I'll be keeping my ears open."

"You've given up on your fishing trips?"

Henry Thomas grimaced. "Sure hated to have to do that. I mean, it was fun while it lasted. But hell, man, I've explored every inch of coastline from here to there, including down into Mexico for a fair distance, and if there's a Harwig ship hidden anywhere between Tampico and Galveston, I can't find the son of a bitch. So I figured to set that aside and see what I could do here. Other than keeping a dumb-ass Pink alive, that is."

"Why, you scrawny little SOB!" Raider retorted, which got a laugh out of Tillman. "But I expect you'll be handy if I need you," Raider added.

Henry Thomas grinned at him. "You won't see me, but I'll be around. I'll find you when I want to talk to you."

"And if I want to talk to you?"

"Look me up and hire me to take you out in the boat again." Henry Thomas chuckled. "Or give me a signal. You won't be able to spot me, o' course, but I'll be there to see."

"A signal?"

"Sure. Like, say, if you want to see me that night, use your left hand to pick your right nostril. If it's an emergency and you got to talk with me right away, use the right hand to pick your left nostril. I'll be watching every minute. Or can't you remember all of that? Should I make it something simpler for you?"

Raider kicked a boot off and threw it at the little Ranger. Tillman ducked it with deceptively quick ease and laughed.

"You better get out of here before I complain to the management about the help bothering the paying guests," Raider said.

"Yeah." Henry Thomas stood. "Serious, Rade, I'll be covering you if they try again."

"*When* they try again," Raider corrected. "I hope."

"I'll stop by tomorrow night and compare notes with you. See if you can learn anything about Harwig's past. It might help."

Raider nodded, and the little man checked carefully to make sure there was no one in the hall to see that he had paid the Pinkerton man a visit, then slipped silently out into the corridor.

Raider kicked his other boot off and prepared for bed. His last thoughts, though, were not about Jon Harwig and this case. They were about Lucy Barnes. Damn, but he missed her. More than he really should.

CHAPTER TWENTY-THREE

"Another lunch on you? Hell yes, I'll go for it," McInally said. He winked. "I c'n be bought, ye know. A good meal or a round o' drinks, an' I'm yer man, Raider." He laughed and led the way into the restaurant.

Raider waited until they had both ordered and the waiter was out of earshot before he brought up the subject that had made him look McInally up today.

"I was doing some thinking while I was laid up," he said, "and there are some things I was hoping you could help me with."

"Anything," the former first mate said. "I told you that already, an' I meant it, son."

"Thanks. Now. . . ." The waiter interrupted by bringing their coffee. When the man was gone again Raider put on a casual expression, as if the questions were entirely routine. "What it is," he said, "is simple background information. I mean, I've been given a fair amount of information about Jon Harwig's shipping activities. But I don't know very much about Jon himself."

"That sorta thing could help you?"

Raider shrugged. "Possibly. Possibly not. You never know. So what I want to do is find out all I can. Then I'll know if it was important or not."

"Yeah, well, lemme see now."

McInally launched into a long and involved description of Jon Harwig and his activities that pretty much paralleled what Henry Thomas Tillman had said the night before, although McInally did not actually call Harwig a saint. Instead the now beached ship's officer told Raider at length what a benefactor Jon Harwig was to the entire community of Rockport, in particular to the seamen who made their homes in the small and near-dying community.

"Why, if it wasn't for Jon, Raider, this whole town woulda dried up an' washed away years ago." He lowered his voice and leaned closer. "Not everybody knows this, Raider, but Jon hasn't been keepin' hardly anything in the way o' profit for himself these past dozen years or so. If he had been, I reckon he'd be in better shape t' hold out now. But he cut 'er t' the bone, he did, just so's he could help ever'body else in this town. That's why he's so bad hurt by these losses. Ever'body thinks a man owns a shippin' line o' fourteen bottoms and all o' them busy plyin' the Gulf waters, why, that man's gotta be rich. Right? Sure that's what ever'body thinks. But it ain't so. Jon coulda been ten, twenty times richer'n he is today if he'd floated with the tide an' moved down t' Corpus or up t' Galveston or even t' N' Orleans. But he didn't wanta do that. His roots was here, same as ours is, and this's where he chose t' stay. He's a big man, Jon Harwig. A fine man. An' every soul in Rockport, nearabout, will do anything they can t' help. Don't you never question that, Raider. Ever' soul here is on your side o' this problem."

"Almost every soul," Raider said, thinking about the unknown, unseen party who had ambushed him that night.

"Every," McInally insisted. "Whoever's behind Jon Harwig's problems, it ain't any man who's local. No sir, not anybody from this town. We all think too highly o' Jon for that t' be possible."

"I gather it wasn't always that way," Raider said mildly, giving the impression that he knew more than he did.

McInally snorted. "Aw, them days is long ago, Raider. Long ago. Jon repented o' his old ways long ago. Besides, all o' that was really nothing but him being so young and maybe drinkin' more than he should've. That's all that was. Why, he swore off the liquor years ago. I haven't seen 'im touch a drop since. Not a drop, Raider. Can't every man do that, but Jon did. Stopped cold an' hasn't touched a drop since."

Now that was interesting, Raider thought. Jon Harwig was a reformed drunk. The reformed part was hardly grounds for anyone to hate the man, but what might he have done when he was *still* a drunk?

"Tell me about those times," Raider suggested.

McInally seemed reluctant. He had time to marshal his thoughts when the waiter brought their food. Raider let it rest while they ate. Later, though, he repeated the question. "I can't guarantee you that it's important," he admitted, "but it might be."

"All right then. But let's take us a walk an' have this chat in private, eh?"

Raider nodded. He paid for their meals, and McInally led the way down to the waterfront, as if the salt air and the vast spread of sky and water made the subject easier for him to handle.

"It's like this," McInally said finally. "Jon was a young man then." The first mate smiled. "As we all were in them days, son. Young an' full o' pep an' the whole world t' conquer. You know how 'tis."

"Yes."

"Well Jon, he was no different from any other young man. The world was out there, an' he wanted all of it. Wanted t' own it all, control it all, set his flag on every sl   n the Gulf waters. Drove himself hard, he did, an' his men almost as hard. But Jon, he was the kind would take on the heaviest burdens himself. Bought himself a run-down old hull and worked day an' night, him and a man named Leonard who was his partner at the time. The two of 'em took up caulking mallets an' buckets of oakum an' tar, an' between them those two rebuilt that sorry old tub an' made 'er seaworthy. More or less. Then Jon found another run-down ol' relic from the Mexican War times. Leonard went to work on her while Jon set off t' sea in the fixed-up hull. It was a scramble, let me tell ye. Jon'd haul anything. Take on any cargo, drive through the worst storms, short-handed an' bull-headed, impossible delivery dates, any damn thing, whatever, if the return was only pennies. An' every penny he got hold of, he put back into his ships.

"Didn't matter how hard the work was or how little the profit. If there was any kind of profit t' be made, Jon made 'er and put the pennies back inta another ship, better rigging, whatever. Expansion, that's what he was after. He wanted it all, an' he'd do anything to get it. All o' it."

McInally paused and stared out toward the sea for a moment. Then he shrugged. "It came to 'im too. But the hard way. Started with that one miserable ship. Then it was two. Four. Eight. Inside three years, him and Leonard had their flag on, oh, I don't recollect the exact number. Couple dozen small ships, anyhow. An' then Jon wanted *better* ships. More wasn't enough for him then. He wanted better'uns too. He was still driving himself, see, an' driving Leonard too.

"Along about that time, Leonard found himself a bride. Prettiest little gal you ever seen. Brought her back here and decided it was time t' settle down an' enjoy what him and Jon had built. Except Jon didn't see it that way. Jon was drinking heavy by then. Had to, I expect, t' push himself like he did. Kept himself going on guts an' rum an' expected Leonard t' do the same. Except Leonard, he didn't have the stomach for that no more. Leonard wanted t' do some living now that the two of them had something t' live off. I happen t' know something about it, Raider, because I was an able-bodied seaman in those days an' sailing on the old *Hester Lucille* when Jon an' Leonard got into a fight.

"T'wasn't a fist fight, y' understand. An argument. We was on our way t' Cedar Key for a load o' lumber consigned to Indianola." McInally smiled sadly off toward the horizon. "Hell, there's a place I haven't so much as thought of in years. Got wiped out by a hurricane a while back an' never rebuilt. Wasn't no need for it by then. It'd been a hide an' tallow port, too, an' when the wind an' the water took it there just wasn't no reason to rebuild. Back then, though, there was a port there an' we was to pick up lumber at Cedar Key, way the hell an' gone the other side o' the Gulf, an' bring it back to Indianola. Anyhow, Jon hadn't been expecting Leonard t' be aboard the *Hester Lucille*. Leonard was supposed to be minding the business while Jon took the flagship out makin' money for them. But there Leonard showed up, wantin' to divert the *Hester Lucille* t' Mobile and pick up some fancy something for his wife.

"Stupid, Jon called that. Waste of time an' crew wages, he said it was. He was pretty drunk at the time, but even so I expect you could make a case for his argument of it. Hell, there'd be a ship scheduled into Mobile soon enough. There always was, y' see. So Jon had himself a point, but Leonard couldn't see it. Whatever the pretty was, he wanted it an' he wanted it right now, an' he figured they'd made enough money that they could afford to divert a ship for a few days so's he could have this thing.

"Well, t' make a long story a touch shorter, the two of 'em fought about this. Got pretty pissed they did, an' they broke up the partnership over it. Loud, arguin' kind of talk it was. But no papers drawn. I expect they was gonna have the papers drawn when they got back t' home port. O' course we all heard the argument—they was havin' it right there on deck where we couldn't'a not heard—but there wasn't anything signed.

"Well, the upshot of it was that the ship never called at Mobile. Jon figured he had the say since he was the sole owner o' the line by then, so we never put in at Mobile. Just laid course across for Cedar Key. Open sea, y' understand. Swung away from the shore an' made straight for Florida. Come into a storm two nights later, an' Leonard was washed away by a breakin' sea. You wouldn't think it to look at it right now, but the Gulf can be a sonuvabitch when it wants to, an' that night it wanted to. Hell, I near went over myself that storm, an' me agile as a monkey back then. Anyhow, we lost Leonard.

"An' Jon, he got to blaming himself an' drinking all the heavier because o' that. Picked up our cargo and carried it t' Indianola, then back home t' Rockport to give the widow the bad news. Then some unthinkin' SOB talked around about the partnership being broke up, which caused hard feelings with the widow, an' she come down on Jon right hard. Accused him o' pushing Leonard overboard, which was just tears talking because I was on that ship an' I happen t' know that Jon was below when Leonard was lost, but she got it in mind that Jon'd had something to do with her man dying, an' she made all kinds o' threats about it. And Jon, he was drunk anyhow and not thinking right, an' he got hot an' kinda nasty right back at her. Turned out the partnership, which'd been drawn up when both Jon an' Leonard was young bachelors, had a clause in it that said if one of 'em died, the other got the whole company as sole owner. An' Jon, he was hot enough that he swore he'd stick with that an' keep it all if the dumb bitch wouldn't quit slandering him like she was. O' course, she was hot enough that she wasn't going to quit." McInally shook his head. "Them two fought off an' on for years after."

Raider was being quiet, but he was damn sure interested in

everything McInally's rambling story was telling him. If anyone had a motive to ruin Jon Harwig, this woman would be it.

Then McInally crushed the theory.

"Fought until the woman died, they did. Kinda rocked Jon when that happened I think. He quit drinking an' quit pushing so hard an' regretted what'd been said on both sides. But by then o' course it was too late to change. Damn pity, too. Jon, he's been a rock for this town, no pun intended, Raider. It's true. He's been a rock all these years. Not a better man on these waters or any other."

Shit, Raider thought. A motive and a suspect right there for the asking. Except that the suspect was dead and long gone, and the motive gone with her.

It had been worth a try, though.

He talked with McInally a while longer, then excused himself and made his way back to the hotel, leaving McInally standing near the wharf staring wistfully out toward a set of sails distantly seen out beyond the low offshore islands. The ship was too far out for her hull to be visible, but the square-rigged sails floated low over the water like a cloud drifting with the wind.

What they were going to need on this one, Raider decided, was for the damned pirates to make another try for him from ambush. Either that or a voluntary confession blurted out of the blue.

And those were a little bit hard to come by.

Raider looked around on his way back to the hotel, but if Henry Thomas Tillman was anywhere near, the little Ranger was so inconspicuous as to be completely invisible. Raider couldn't spot him, anyhow.

CHAPTER TWENTY-FOUR

If the pirates were going to make another attempt to kill him, Raider reasoned, they would likely wait until after dark to do it, when they would have the night to hide behind.

On the other hand, why the hell should they *bother* trying to kill him? As far as he could tell, he was no threat to them. Or to anyone else, damn it.

He was beginning to feel as though every time he had a direction to go in he found himself in a blind canyon.

Look for a suspect with a motive, find the perfect one and—poof!—it all evaporated into thin air.

Damn!

Still, they had tried it once. With luck they just might be dumb enough to try it again. He was hoping for that but not really expecting anything to happen until nightfall.

He had a few beers, asked questions that were freely answered but provided no real help, and wandered back down to the wharf to watch with a bunch of local loafers while the Harwig coaster *Honoria* was warped to the dock with hawsers and sweat after she overshot the wind and had to submit to the indignity of being dragged home those last few chains. It wasn't the sort of display Raider would have bought tickets to see, but it was the best entertainment Rockport had to offer.

Henry Thomas Tillman, he noticed, was a face in the same crowd of onlookers. The little Ranger seemed to be paying no attention to Raider or anyone else in particular and was there to give a hand wrapping a cable around a bollard. The Tall Man didn't *seem* to be doing a good job or shadowing Raider, which probably meant that he was doing it very well indeed.

Satisfied, Raider went back to the hotel for supper.

He wondered rather idly if Henry Thomas Tillman really would come running if Raider were to pick his nose in public. He grinned to himself at the thought but didn't want to test it out. Hell, he had nothing important to discuss with the Ranger. Not yet. And Henry Thomas would stop by the hotel room sometime later.

In the meantime, Raider had a promise to keep to Lucy Barnes. She would be home from work by now, probably having her dinner. He could see the Tall Man later. Lucy now. He paid for his meal and went back outside.

While he had been eating the sun had set, and it was coming dark. There was no sign now of Tillman, but Raider knew the little man would be out there somewhere in the deepening shadows.

And if he wasn't, well, Raider hadn't gotten to this age by needing his hand held.

He turned down the side street that led to Lucy Barnes's town house.

He was alert to the possibility of trouble, but the streets were silent and the shadows empty, the better class of Rockport residents apparently indoors at this hour.

Raider's steps quickened as he neared Lucy's home, and his thoughts jumped forward to the way she felt in his arms— and elsewhere—the way she would feel pressed against him again in just a matter of moments. He lengthened his stride even more and hurried toward the gate in the white-painted picket fence.

"Down!"

The voice from the shadows was quietly urgent.

Raider dropped, his hand sweeping the Remington out, and even before he hit the ground there was a sharp, brittle crack as a small-caliber revolver spat lead close enough to Raider's head that he could hear the quick-zipping drone of the bullet passing close to his left ear.

There was a grunt of pain from the crotch of a shaggy old pecan tree, and a shotgun disgorged a gout of flame and lead into the ground.

The SOB had been waiting up in the tree, not down on the ground where Raider would have expected him to be. There was nothing seen in the shadows because there was no one down there to see.

Raider's return fire was instant.

The big Remington was already in his hand, needing only a target on which to vent his fury.

The big gun roared, and the man in the tree slumped forward, dropping the sawed-off scattergun and following it to the ground. The body hit with a limp, raw-meat finality that said the would-be assassin was dead.

The gunman had guessed where Raider would go—or there were others posted around town in the places where Raider might travel—because he was inside Lucy's yard, hiding in the pecan tree that shaded her front porch.

Raider jumped over the low fence and approached the fallen gunman with caution but with no real concern. He knew perfectly well that the man was dead. No one could fall like that, so completely limp and loose, while he retained the least spark of life in his body.

The shotgun lay half underneath the body, one barrel still loaded and lethal. But the man who had wanted to use it was past that or any other impulse.

Raider looked around, but there were no other ambushers. Nor was there any sign whatsoever of Henry Thomas Tillman.

It was Tillman who had warned him, who had fired that first shot. At the critical moment, the Tall Man had been across the street from Raider and from the ambusher, and Raider had walked between Tillman and his target.

The Ranger remained as completely hidden now, though, as he had been ever since Raider left the hotel on his way here. Not once had the tall Pinkerton gotten the first hint of the little man's presence.

Raider rubbed his chin and automatically, without conscious thought, punched the empty cartridge case out of the cylinder of his Remington and reloaded by feel in the dark before he dropped the weapon back into his holster.

By now the sound and the fury of the attack, the gunshots and the grunts of pain, were causing concern behind the closed doors and lighted windows of the houses nearby. Raider could hear cautious, tentatively offered questions coming from behind curtained windows.

Oddly enough, it was Lucy Barnes who first gained the courage to come outside and see what had happened in this quiet, dignified neighborhood.

She appeared in the doorway of her home, bright yellow

lamplight flooding out onto the porch from behind her and outlining her slim body in silhouette.

"What . . . what happened?" she asked hesitantly.

"It's all right, Lucy," Raider reassured her. "It will be all right now."

When she heard his voice she ran to him and held him close, rising on tiptoes to kiss him and clutch herself tight against his chest. "You're all right, dear? Are you hurt?" She was trembling and obviously worried.

"I'm fine," he said. "Just fine." He returned her kiss briefly, then said, "Go back inside, honey. I don't want you t' see this. Send Conchita out with a lantern if you would, but you stay inside. I'll be in when I can."

Her eyes grew wide. "You mean . . . again? Someone tried to shoot you again?" She looked as though she might cry.

Then her expression hardened and, surprising Raider in the intensity of her emotion, she pulled away from him and walked beneath the pecan to stand over the body of the dead ambusher.

"You . . . !" She seemed at a loss for words powerful enough to express her disgust. Instead she spat angrily down at the body of the dead man, gasped at the enormity of it all, and turned to run back into the house.

"Well, I'll be go to hell," Raider whispered to himself.

He had not had any idea at all that Lucy Barnes felt so powerfully toward him. It was damned flattering, he had to admit that, but also worrisome. He hoped the lady was not expecting more attachment than he was willing—able—to give her.

Lucy never did remember to send the lantern out, but within a few minutes some of the braver neighbors poked their heads outside, and a few minutes after that a boy was dispatched to fetch the town marshal, and a crowd of the curious was growing as men and boys sought to get a better look at the blood and the corpse and the shotgun.

There was a babble of questions and comments, but Raider paid no attention until the marshal got there, then he explained the situation as briefly and as clearly as he could in a voice that held no emotion. He was reporting the crime, but he was thinking about Lucy Barnes and her unexpected reaction to the murder attempt.

The town marshal, an ineffectual man who used to run a

now closed tallow factory, turned the body over and called for a light to be held closer. "Anybody know this man?"

No one did.

Except Raider. He remembered him. He had been one of the pirates who boarded and took the *Henrietta*. The pirate had been wearing a mustache then and was clean-shaven now, but Raider was positive this was one of the pirates. He told the marshal that.

The marshal, a man named Dowling, grunted and examined the corpse. "You say you shot once?"

Raider shook his head. "Once, twice, to tell you the truth, Marshal, I guess I don't remember so well, it all happened so fast," Raider lied.

He could see as well as anyone that there were two wounds on the body. One—it would have been Raider's shot—had struck the man square in the chest. That would have been the shot that instantly killed him. The other wound—smaller, although with luck the marshal would not have experience enough to recognize and comment on that fact—was a disabling but certainly not lethal small-caliber gunshot high on the point of the man's shoulder.

"I just don't remember for certain sure, Marshal," Raider repeated.

"I heard three shots," a voice from the crowd piped up.

Raider looked around. Henry Thomas Tillman was there, just another bystander in the crowd craning his scrawny neck to get a better view and blending in with the others whose clothes said they were not residents of this neighborhood but had been drawn here after the fact to share in the excitement.

"That could be," Raider said. "I'm pretty sure he got one barrel off before I got him."

"You were lucky, Pinkerton man. One barrel could cut a mule in half outa a thing like that."

One of the onlookers reached down to pick up the shotgun, but the marshal stopped him. "Don't, Ike. I'll do that."

"Yes, sir." The townsman stepped back, and Dowling picked up the stubby, ugly, devastatingly effective weapon. Dowling held the thing gingerly, like a man who was not overly familiar with firearms and was at least half frightened of them.

The shotgun was of modern design, not one of the old but still common muzzle-loaders. Dowling had to fumble for a moment before he was able to find the under-action lever that opened the breech. He removed the two shells from the chambers and grunted again. "He got one off, all right. One fired and the other not." He looked at Raider. "You was lucky, young fella."

"Yeah."

The marshal snapped the action of the shotgun closed and dropped both shells into his pocket. He looked around at the crowd. "No one knows who this man is? Where he comes from?"

No one admitted knowledge of the dead man.

Raider borrowed the whale oil lamp someone had carried from a nearby house and bent closer to the dead man. But there was nothing he could add to Dowling's limited information. Raider had seen the man as a pirate aboard the *Henrietta* but never on the streets of Rockport.

"Sorry," he said.

"I'll circulate a description tomorrow. Someone must know who he is. Was. We'll find out sooner or later."

Raider had scant faith in that prediction, but he said nothing about it.

"Meanwhile, there's nothing more to be done here tonight," Dowling said.

He designated half a dozen men to carry the body away and draped the shotgun over his own arm.

It amused Raider to note that the marshal had been looking in the direction of Henry Thomas Tillman when he began appointing men to the body removal detail. But by the time Dowling spoke, the little loafer was no longer part of that particular crowd.

Dowling shooed the crowd off toward their homes or their saloons—Raider suspected the drinking establishments of Rockport would do a fine business this night—and paused to say to Raider, "I expect there's no secret what this was all about, o' course. But if you insist on getting yourself shot, young man, I wish you'd do it someplace else."

Raider laughed. "If it's all the same to you, Marshal, I'd ruther not do it at all."

"That's fine with me, son, but I ain't the one you got to convince. Tell it to them that's after you."

The laughter disappeared, and Raider's expression became

hard. "That, sir, is something I do intend to do. Now if you'll excuse me?"

He turned away and headed toward Lucy's front door. She had been badly shaken by the violence in her yard. She needed comforting. He intended to see that she got it.

CHAPTER TWENTY-FIVE

"You look tuckered," Henry Thomas Tillman said with a grin.

"Why, you little sonuvabitch. You've been peeking again."

"Not at the, uh, critical moments," the Tall Man said. He tossed his hat onto the foot of Raider's bed and stretched out with his hands laced behind his neck. "Busy night," he observed.

"Yeah. And thanks. I hadn't been looking for them in the damn trees like that."

"To tell you the truth, I hadn't either. I didn't spot him until he moved to bring that scattergun to bear. And then you were right in the way." Henry Thomas chuckled. "Got kinda busy for a minute there. But I sure wish you hadn't shot him. I was sure wanting to have a word with the man."

"Now Henry Thomas, you aren't gonna lie there and tell me you deliberately popped him in the shoulder, are you?"

"Of course I did. What the hell do you think!"

"At night? Across the street and half the yard? With a popgun like that?"

Tillman smiled.

Raider shook his head. "I swear I thought you'd missed your shot. And when that shotgun went off . . ."

"Oh, I don't blame you. I might have done the same thing myself. But it's still a shame."

"I guess you heard me tell the marshal that the guy was one of the pirates who took the *Henrietta*."

Henry Thomas nodded. "Also that nobody around here claims to've seen the man before tonight. Does that strike you odd?"

"It does. So does something else I noticed about him."

Tillman raised an eyebrow.

"Did you happen to notice his feet?"

"Actually," Henry Thomas said dryly, "I was concentrating elsewhere at the time."

"I mean afterward." It was Raider's turn to grin. Apparently he had spotted something that had slipped past the Tall Man.

Henry Thomas Tillman thought about it for a moment, then shrugged.

"The guy was wearing boots," Raider said. "Stockman's boots. With Mexican rowel spurs. How often do you see boots and spurs on board a ship?"

"I'll be damned," Tillman said. "But now that you mention it, he was. I never noticed, I guess, because most everybody I usually deal with wears boots and spurs all the time."

"Of course they do in your line of work. And in most of mine, for that matter. But I remarked on it because it seems so funny to me around here where hardly anybody wears them."

"And when I'm not on the job I'm generally around the water, so that doesn't strike me as odd either. It's a matter of what you expect to see when you're one place or the other."

"Wherever the guy came from tonight," Raider said, "he rode a horse. He didn't get here on any boat."

"But pirates don't . . ."

Raider grinned again. "Pirates don't go fogging after their quarry on horseback, do they? Like road agents after a stagecoach or something."

"Interesting," Tillman said. "I don't know what the hell it means, but it's interesting, all right. Of course everybody in this country rides. Except by water that's about the only way to get around."

"But not everybody in this country wears hand-stitched stockman's boots. In fact, that's a pretty damned seldom item in Rockport."

"Now if we just knew what it meant . . ." Henry Thomas said, his voice tailing away.

"Yeah." Raider sighed. "Actually, I was kinda hoping you'd have some ideas on the subject, being closer to the local way of thinking than me."

"I'll chew on it, but nothing comes to mind right off."

"Me neither." Raider leaned forward. "Drink?"

"A beer would be nice."

"I could have a keg sent up. Or would a whiskey do?"

"The whiskey'll be fine."

Raider had only one glass in the hotel room, so he gave it to his guest and took a swallow from the bottle for himself.

"We need a break in this thing, Raider. We need to set one of those bastards up for another try and *this* time take him alive. But I don't want to come out in the open backing you up."

"I think . . . give me a minute to work this out. But I think I'm commencing to get some ideas on that, Henry Thomas."

"Take your time. But pass that bottle while you're doing it."

CHAPTER TWENTY-SIX

The word must have gotten around that Raider and Mrs. Barnes were keeping company, because this time when Raider showed up at the chandlery the old fossil who clerked downstairs was grudgingly polite, and when Raider climbed the staircase to the office, Lucy's secretary was all smiles and welcome. "You can go right in, Mr. Raider."

He thanked the woman and tapped lightly on Lucy's door.

"Come in." She sounded brisk and businesslike, something he had quite forgotten about her after the past week or so.

A frown of concentration changed immediately to a smile of warm welcome when she saw who her visitor was. She dropped a pencil onto the papers that littered her desk and ran to greet him with a hug and a kiss hungry enough to have no place in an office setting.

"Whoa," he said, although he was pleased by the reaction. "Someone might see in."

"I could draw the blinds," she whispered against his mouth.

"Mmmm. Don't tempt me." He could feel her hands between their bodies, stroking and caressing and bringing him to quick arousal. The door to the outer office was not completely closed, damn it, and if *she* wasn't worried about her reputation, *he* was. He pulled away from her and turned to set the latch quietly.

Lucy giggled and went to pull roller blinds down over the large window that looked down onto the sales floor.

"Lucy!"

"Raider, dear." She laughed. "You look positively shocked."

He felt his cheeks growing warmer. He couldn't hardly believe it himself, but he *felt* positively shocked. He thought he had outgrown such feelings half a lifetime ago.

"If anything, dear, my friends here will be happy for me. And if anyone is not my friend, well, I shan't care a fig what they might think anyhow." She began undoing the row of tiny, pearly buttons that held her bodice closed.

Raider looked rather wildly about. There was no provision made in this office for daytime assignations behind closed doors. No couch or daybed or . . . anything.

Still laughing, and now quite fetchingly naked, Lucy solved the problem by sweeping her paperwork to the floor and lying on top of the wide, polished surface of her desk, presenting herself to him, offering herself totally.

Raider began hurriedly undoing buckles and buttons of his own. It would, after all, have been unkind to do otherwise.

"What I actually came here for," he said somewhat later, when the breathing had returned to normal and the sweat was drying on his bare chest—hers too, for that matter—"was to ask a favor of you."

"Of course, darling. Anything."

He grinned at the pretty woman, even lovelier now in the flushed afterglow of pleasure. "Okay. Thanks." He stood and reached for his trousers.

Lucy yelped with surprise. "Where are you going?"

"Why, I'm going out. I have things to do, ma'am. And you said it was okay." He gave her a wide-eyed look of feigned innocence.

"But aren't you even going to tell me . . . I mean, you haven't even told me what favor you *want*, dear."

"No need," he said glibly. "You already told me I could do it."

"But . . ." Lucy blinked and sat up. She looked genuinely confused.

Then Raider began to laugh, and she gave him a mock frown as she realized he had been teasing her.

He bent to kiss her. Then to touch her. And the touching led to more touching, and that led to something further, so that it was actually quite a while later before he got around to explaining the favor she had already granted.

And after all, he reasoned, he wasn't really wasting the time he was spending with the widow Barnes.

He had to give Henry Thomas Tillman time to get himself into position, didn't he?

CHAPTER TWENTY-SEVEN

Raider was deliberately conspicuous about looking for a place where he could rent a horse, even though he already knew that the only livery in town was a run-down affair housed in one of the former tallow factories at the west end of town.

He asked several different people for advice in the matter and made sure he was very much visible when he finally did walk to the livery.

Jon Harwig's pirates had to be getting information from some source in Rockport itself, possibly Harwig himself or possibly someone else, but with certainty from someone in the town, and Raider's plan with Henry Thomas Tillman called for that unknown someone to learn that the Pinkerton search for the criminals was extending into the countryside and not necessarily just along the shoreline.

If the pirates were concerned about his snooping—and they damn sure had to be or they wouldn't have staged the two ambush attempts on his life—they would be doubly concerned about his looking for them away from the coast.

It was the evidence of the boots and spurs on the dead man from the pecan tree that suggested the trap, intended to drive the pirates out into the open finally.

One drawback was that Henry Thomas, posing here as a harmless drifter known as Tom Henry, did not have the freedom to hire a horse for himself. And the little Ranger's own horses were way the hell south at his home base near Brownsville. The Tall Man had arrived in Rockport by boat, of course, with no idea that he might need ground transportation for the job.

So Raider had had to while away a considerable amount of time today while Henry Thomas hiked to the point where Raider had agreed to meet him.

Raider smiled to himself when he thought about the way that delaying time had been spent.

When he reached the lone livery serving Rockport, he was disappointed. Saddle horses were not much in demand at this seaport, and the pickings were damned slim. Almost nonexistent, in fact.

"I'll take that bony blue gelding," he said after looking over the available mounts. "And I'll need a pack animal, too."

"Did ye say you want th' bonny blue roan, mister?" the hostler asked with a chuckle.

Raider made a face. Anyone who called such a sway-backed bag of bones "bonny" was either a fool or a jokester. And the hostler was elderly but did not look much like a fool.

The hostler laughed again and fetched the ugly roan out of the pen while Raider selected from the assortment of saddles available for hire with the horses. There were two of them, actually. Raider took the lesser of the two evils between them.

"Only got one animul that'll pack," the hostler said without any note of apology. "An' I got no pack frame. Would ye settle for t'other saddle? Ye can drape yer pack goods over it, I should think."

Raider quickly agreed. Actually, the lack of a pack frame was a bonus as far as he was concerned, and would be considered even more so by Henry Thomas. Since Raider could not reasonably hire two horses with saddles, they had expected to ditch the pack frame somewhere and make Henry Thomas ride bareback. The Tall Man would bless him for this good fortune.

Or maybe not.

Raider had to hide a grin when he saw the "pack animul" the hostler dragged out of the corral.

The beast was a mule, with a backbone sharp enough to slice cheese and a hide that looked pre-tanned and already chewed by rats.

The hostler said the mule was trained to carry a pack. But the man hadn't mentioned a thing about its ability to pack a man on its back. Ol' Henry Thomas would just have to climb aboard and hope for the best when the time came. If nothing else, though, this experience could be damned amusing. For a spectator.

Raider stifled his smiles and paid the liveryman a week's hire for both animals.

"Be gone that long, eh?"

Raider shrugged. "Can't ever be sure. If it turns out to be longer, don't worry about it. I'm good for it."

"Oh, I ain't worried," the hostler assured him. "If you don't come back I c'n always bill the Pinkerton Agency direct." He didn't mention the ambush attacks directly, but it was plain that he had heard about them, along with everyone else in Rockport.

Raider winked at him. "I'll be back."

The hostler helped him saddle the two animals, and Raider rode back to the hotel with the mule trailing placidly at the end of a lead rope.

Raider hoped to hell he never had to chase the pirates down on horseback. Or for that matter that he ever had to run from anybody.

Some horses have as their strong point speed. Others endurance. Still others an ability to outthink a cow, and so on.

After half an hour in the saddle, Raider had concluded that the blue roan's forte in life had to be something to do with the production of glue.

The beast was slow, easily fatigued, and just plain stupid.

It could not maintain a gait or a direction without constant attention from its rider and would booger and go wildly spooky at the merest hint of a leaf blowing across the ground under its nose. Twice the fool creature had damn near unseated him when sleepy somnolence jumped without warning into instant panic at the flutter of some imagined ghost lurking in the salt grass beside the sandy twin tracks of the road south. One of those times it was only the placid presence of the mule, acting as an anchor at its end of the lead rope, that kept the mottled roan from becoming a runaway.

When Raider reached his destination he was greeted by a horselaugh and by the sight of the Tall Man reclining in the shade. By that time Raider was in no mood to see the humor in the situation.

"You can certainly pick 'em," Henry Thomas said cheerfully.

Raider scowled at the little man.

Tillman's response was another outburst of laughter.

"You won't laugh so damn loud when you crawl on top of the mule," Raider said. Reminding himself of Henry Thomas's coming discomfort made him feel a little better about the shortcomings of his own mount. At least he wouldn't have to suffer that indignity. Henry Thomas only laughed again, though, and after a moment Raider smiled too. "Come on, then. You can help me unload some of this junk."

He had deliberately bought a number of bulky, mostly useless goods, just so he would have an excuse to be dragging a pack animal behind him. Now most of the surplus articles could be discarded and the saddled mule turned over to the Tall Man.

Henry Thomas was still chuckling when he got to his feet and came out into the sunshine to begin unloading the bags that were tied over the mule's saddle.

CHAPTER TWENTY-EIGHT

Raider was tired, bored, and becoming more than a little worried. Three days now he had spent in the saddle making a target of himself.

And no one had come out to play.

That was the discouraging part of it.

Each day he had been in the saddle shortly after dawn, after giving Henry Thomas Tillman a start of more than an hour so the little man could slip away in the dark to take up his position as shadow, and no one had yet taken so much as a passing interest in him.

The few people he met on the road, mostly farmers or the occasional vaquero, nodded politely and once in a while stopped to pass the time.

But no one, no one at all, seemed remotely interested in shooting Raider in the back.

That was damned well disappointing, it was.

He had gone out to get shot at, damn it. So why was no one taking him up on the offer?

Now he was back at his temporary base—Lucy's beach house.

"I don't get it," Raider admitted glumly to the little Texas Ranger.

"What the hell," Tillman said with a shrug. "You getting paid by the job instead of the hour?"

"It's just that I figured . . . we figured . . ."

"So their information is slow. Hell, Rade, that tells us something too, maybe. If their communications are slow, maybe their contact in Rockport isn't local exactly but more like a traveling salesman who comes through town once a week, something like that."

"It's a possibility," Raider said without believing it.

"We'll give it some more time. If nothing happens pretty soon you can go back to town and start looking into the drummers who come through on a regular basis. People like that. One of them could be our break. Drink?"

"Sure." Raider sighed. "At least we're living high on the hog for being a pair of failures."

Henry Thomas Tillman grinned and crossed the parlor to the liquor cabinet. The cabinet was well stocked with expensive brandies and liqueurs, more to Tillman's palate than Raider's. The little man had been systematically sampling the offerings, although never so heavily that it showed.

"Do you figure the owner'll show up this weekend?" Tillman asked as he poured two glasses of French brandy from a dust-caked bottle.

"She said she'd stay away if I wasn't back to let her know it was safe to come out for the weekend."

"I don't want to take any chances on her seeing me here. It's one thing for the lady to know you're using the place. No need in tipping her to me, too." He held up a hand before Raider could protest. "I know what you're fixing to say. It isn't her I'm worried about. Anybody can make a slip. Like she might mention something to the fella that looks after the place. Hell, he already knows you're here. He could tell someone who shouldn't hear it. Come to that, I hope he does. But I don't want him spilling anything about the *second* gringo who's camping out in the widow's guest room."

Raider nodded. As usual, Tillman's reasoning was sound. Lucy might well think nothing about mentioning Henry Thomas to a trusted employee, even if she were warned to be quiet about it. Better not to take the risk than to depend on someone else's judgment.

Henry Thomas handed Raider his glass, then returned to his chair in a shadowy corner of the parlor. The porch where Lucy liked to work at her paintings when she was at the beach house was actually much more comfortable, but it was too open for any hope of privacy. Too much chance that the presence of the second occupant of the house could be seen and noted.

"I . . ." Raider began, then stopped as Tillman quickly set

his glass down on the floor behind the chair, where it would not likely be noticed, and seemed to disappear, drifting swiftly and noiselessly into the hall.

A moment later Raider too heard the warning sounds that had sent Henry Thomas into hiding.

Someone was approaching the house. Raider could hear the muted grinding sound of footsteps on sand.

Raider's hand crept toward the Remington at his waist. This could be what they had been hoping for.

"Señor?" the voice called politely out of the night.

"In the parlor, Estevan."

Raider heard a creak of floorboards behind him and knew that Tillman had heard and would be well out of sight. A moment later he could hear Estevan mounting the steps to the porch and letting himself inside. The slender peon came down the hallway where Henry Thomas had just been and came into the parlor with his wide-brimmed sombrero held nervously in front of him.

"Yes, Estevan?" The man had to have some good reason for being here. He hadn't come near the place since Raider delivered Lucy's message that her guest was to be allowed undisturbed use of the house.

"For you, señor." Estevan reached inside his shirt—and came rather close to getting himself shot, although he probably never realized it—and brought out a rumpled and dirt-smudged envelope. "From the señora," he said. "For your hand only. Her man give it to me so he does not be seen coming to this place himself, eh?"

Raider nodded and accepted the envelope. The flap was sealed with wax, and a signet ring impression had been made in it. Raider had not seen the seal before but he assumed it would be Lucy's from the twined L.B. initials that were part of the design.

"Thanks, Estevan."

"*Buenas noches,* señor." The peon bobbed his head and backed out of the room. Raider heard him leave with quick, scurrying footsteps, as if he was pleased to be rid of an uncomfortable chore. Probably, Raider decided, because of the conflict between the need to deliver a note now and the earlier instructions to stay away while Raider was here.

"What is it?" Tillman's voice came from the doorway Estevan had just vacated. The little man reappeared as silently as he had vanished only moments earlier.

"Give me a second. I haven't opened it yet."

"Smart of the lady to not send somebody direct to the house," Tillman observed while Raider broke the brittle seal and extracted a single sheet of expensive notepaper.

"Yeah," Raider said absently. Then, "Aw, shit," as he read the brief note.

He scowled and handed the paper to the Tall Man.

"Yeah. Shit," the Tall Man agreed.

The note read: "Dear; Thought you should know at once. Another Harwig ship is overdue in port. A wire received from Palacios indicates sighting of men marooned on Matagorda Island, possibly the crew from the *Haverford*. A rescue boat has been sent for them. Forgive me for bothering you if this is not important. I miss you. Love, L."

Raider frowned. "At least we know now why the damn pirates haven't been interested in backshooting me the past few days."

"Yeah. The sons o' bitches have been busy working elsewhere."

"I suppose I better get back to town and hold Harwig's hand," Raider said. "We'll try this again in a couple days."

Tillman winked at him. "Remember, Rade. Pick your nose if you need me. Otherwise I'll see you in your room some dark night."

"You do that."

"And don't forget to take the mule with you. I'll walk back." It was going to be a long hike, but at least he had the darkness and the cool of the night to make the trip more comfortable this time.

"Yeah. See you in town," Raider said.

CHAPTER TWENTY-NINE

The rescue craft out of Palacios reached Rockport shortly after dawn the next day. Raider was among the men and women who were gathered at the wharf to meet them, alerted by signal flags aboard the beamy fishing vessel that had taken the men off Matagorda and brought them home.

Jon Harwig was at Raider's side, wringing his hands as he had done for much of the night. At least in public the man had quit moaning about his financial problems. Raider had been listening to that all through the hours of darkness, and neither he nor Harwig had gotten any sleep while they waited for the Palacios trawler to be sighted.

The one thing the vigil had accomplished was to convince Raider at least to his own satisfaction that Jon Harwig could not be masterminding the piracy of his own boats. No one could fake that much anguish for so long a period.

"I hope my men are all right. I hope for at least that much," Harwig said in a voice made hoarse by a night of nearly nonstop talking.

"We'll know soon enough," Raider said calmly. The fishing boat was within a few rods of the wharf now.

There were plenty of hands eager to grab the hawsers and snug the tubby fisherman to the pilings. Raider noticed that, as before, the Tall Man was inconspicuously part of the crowd of helpers. Tillman looked none the worse for his night of walking except for needing a shave.

"Those are your men, aren't they?" Raider asked.

Harwig nodded. His expression was one of thorough misery. It grew even more miserable when the first man ashore had to be carried. The sailor's face and hands were heavily bandaged.

"Oh, Jesus," Harwig groaned. "Tim Laycock's been wounded."

There was a gabble of noise as everyone tried to ask questions at once. Gradually their story became clear.

The Harwig ship *Haverford*, flagship and pride of the line, was lured to the pirates by a false distress signal and boarded by men who had looked like the victims of a shipboard fire. The phony victim was a fishing boat much like the one from Palacios. Once the pirates were aboard the *Haverford*, the fishing boat was deliberately scuttled and allowed to sink. One of the *Haverford* crewmen had gotten a look at the sinking boat's nameplate. It was the *Albacore Lady* out of Corpus Cristi. Raider tucked that knowledge away to be checked out later.

His own opinion was that no outfit subject to the piracy that was plaguing the Harwig ships should have been damnfool enough to approach another boat, any other boat, while at sea, regardless of the circumstances.

Raider seemed to be the only man in the crowd who held that opinion, though.

"No seaman could ignore a flare, mister. No man o' the sea could do that. Never," was the way a man in the crowd explained it.

Laycock had been wounded when he tried to resist the boarders, whose wounds were fake, seemingly charred flesh, which proved later to be only charcoal smeared on arms and faces.

Laycock, it seemed, offered resistance, trying to wrestle with one of the pirates and disarm him. The young man was burned when the pirate's shotgun fired, the powder flash of the discharge searing his cheek and hands.

"Interestin' thing 'bout it," the *Haverford*'s captain reported to his boss, "was the larruping that boy got, the one as fired 'is shotgun."

"What's that?" Raider asked.

The captain, a man named Quint, ignored the question until Harwig made introductions and told him to cooperate with the Pinkerton operative. Then he was eager enough to explain.

"Damnedest thing," Quint explained then. "Me, I can't

figger it much. After the scuffle, y' see, young Laycock was floppin' on the deck, wallerin' from side to side an' cryin' from the hurt of it, an' the pirate cap'n, first thing he done was to detail a pair o' his boys t' tend to Tim. Then he took the shotgun away from the lad as done the deed. Snatched that gun right away from him an' flung it over the side. Then wi' his own fists he proceeded to beat hell outa that boy, cussin' him fearful an' allowin' that he knowed better an'd never sail with'em ag'in if ever he done such a trick a second time.

"An' the way they tended Laycock? Why, 'twas them that bandaged 'im an' put salve on 'is burns an' treated 'im as tender as his own mother could've."

Captain Quint went on in that vein for some time. And later, when Raider talked to others of the *Haverford*'s crew, the story was repeated over and over again with the same degree of amazement at the concern the pirates had shown for the injured seaman, and at the severity of the beating the pirate captain had given his own man.

Apparently by the time the captain got done with the fellow he was unable to work and was taken below decks, not to be seen again while the crew of the *Haverford* remained aboard.

The crew of the stolen ship was taken to a desolate stretch on the seaward side of Matagorda and left there with water and provisions enough to last them a week, even though it was as good as a certainty that they would be spotted the first day. They were even given the *Haverford*'s semaphore flags to make certain they would be able to contact the first ship or boat that passed.

"I never knew pirates were so generous to their victims," Raider observed at one point.

"I didn't either," Harwig admitted. "But then these are the only pirates I've ever had experience with."

Raider grunted and turned away. The excitement was over, the *Haverford* crew safely home, although without their ship.

It seemed truly strange, though, that the pirates would be so solicitous of their victims.

There probably was a valuable clue in that bit of information, although Raider was damned if he could see what it might be.

He put the thought aside for the moment when he saw Lucy and several of her employees standing at the entrance to the chandlery. She looked as concerned as everyone else about the crew of the *Haverford*.

Her face was wanly pale, and she seemed distracted when she greeted him. "Is someone hurt? It looks like one of those young men was hurt."

Raider explained the situation and squeezed her hand. She seemed a little calmer after that, but she kept glancing off toward the crowd on the wharf until Laycock was helped away toward his parents' home.

Finally she sighed and attempted a smile. She leaned closer to Raider and whispered, "I've missed you."

"You ain't the only one, lady."

"Do you have time to come upstairs?"

He smiled at her. "If I didn't, I'd make time."

"You may go to breakfast now," she said to her secretary, who was among the gawkers clustered at the doorway. "And Wallace, please see that Mr. Raider and I are not disturbed."

"Yes'm, Miz Barnes." The old buzzard who had been so snippy with Raider on his first visit here looked serious but not at all disapproving. Raider got the impression that Generals Crook and Terry with all their troops would not be able to get past Wallace until or unless Lucy Barnes gave permission for them to pass.

Lucy led the way up to the office. By the time they reached the privacy of her closed doors she seemed her own sweet, desirable self. She came into Raider's arms with a moan of anticipation, and for a while there he wouldn't have cared if the pirates sailed into Aransas Bay and carried off the entire town behind his back.

CHAPTER THIRTY

"All right," Henry Thomas Tillman said crisply. "So we don't know everything. Yet. We do know more now than we did. We know where the pirates were when we were trying to trap them. They were out taking the *Haverford*. And we know that for some reason they're uncommonly worried about not letting the crews of the stolen boats come to harm. That has to be something." Tillman was pacing up and down the length of Raider's hotel room. For a change Raider was being allowed the use of his own bed while they talked and was stretched out on it with a pair of pillows propped behind his back.

"Sure it tells us something," Raider agreed. "But what?"

The little man grinned. "Damned if I know. I figure it's your turn to say something." Tillman was a long way from handsome, but he was a likable little cuss, Raider decided.

Raider sat up and rubbed at his chin. "I say we let that stew a while and go back to our original idea. Set those boys up with me as bait an' have at 'em when they show themselves." He smiled. "But I sure wish I wasn't always the one has to act as target."

"Come to think of it," Tillman said, "they aren't shy about shooting down visiting Pinks, are they? Just those sailor boys."

"Because they're seamen themselves, likely," Raider suggested.

"Maybe." Henry Thomas sounded skeptical about it, though. That was reasonable enough. Raider was not convinced himself, but that was the only explanation he could think of for the difference of harmful intentions.

"We should give them a day or two to get settled wherever it is they go after these capers," Raider said, "and to hear that I'm prowling the countryside on horseback. That should bring them outa the woodwork, once they do hear it."

Tillman nodded. "I sure as hell wish we could find out what they're doing with those ships. Believe me, I've sailed this coast till I know every creek and cranny from here to there and back again. I can't find a damn thing. Not even down into Mexico, which was what I figured when I first got onto this. But not a peep. And I have me some pretty good informers down that side of the border. Nobody's heard a thing."

"About that or any other thing," Raider grumped. "We just aren't . . ."

"Yeah," Tillman agreed sourly.

"Tell you what," Raider said. "I'm going to spend the weekend down at the beach house with Lucy. I'll take the horse and mule down with me and just stay there when she comes back to town Sunday night. You hang in here and see what your ears bring you. You can meet me down there any time after she drives off Sunday evening. And while you're at it, you might check with your people and see if there are any leads from the Corpus end. That's where the fishing boat was from. The—what was it?—*Albacore Lady*. It was probably stolen, like the *Cockleshell* was, but it needs to be checked, just to make sure."

"I'll take a little sail tomorrow and get a wire off to my captain," Tillman said. "Even in the Rangers we have our share of pencil pushers. But this is the sort of thing they can do quick and easy where it'd take me a week to ride down to Corpus and check it out myself. I might even know something by the time I see you Sunday night."

"All right. We're agreed," Raider said. "I'll meet you at the beach house on Sunday."

Henry Thomas Tillman gave him a grin and a wink.

"And damn you, don't you be doing any peeking this time. A man oughta be entitled to some privacy."

The little Ranger laughed but made no promises. "Sunday," he said as he slipped out the door into the empty hallway.

CHAPTER THIRTY-ONE

Lucy pressed herself against him and gave him a lingering kiss. When finally she stepped back away from him she seemed sad. She stroked his cheek and sighed.

Raider smiled at her. "It's only for a few days, you know."

She sighed again. "I know. I just..." She shook her head, leaving the thought unspoken.

"Go on now," he urged. "I've already kept you here past dark. If you have any trouble on the road, why, I won't be able to forgive myself. You go on now. I'll see you again soon as I can."

She grasped his hand with a fierce, sudden strength, then turned and literally ran out to the waiting carriage.

Raider watched her go with mixed emotions. He was anxious for Henry Thomas Tillman to get here so they could get back to the task at hand. But damn, he missed her already. She was rapidly becoming something...special. He wouldn't allow himself to think of his feelings in any terms more definite than that. But he couldn't stop himself from feeling the things he was feeling.

He stood in the doorway watching until she had the rig moving at a brisk trot. The carriage with its precious cargo disappeared around the side of the house toward the road, and he tried to make himself not worry about her. The horse was reliable and knew the way. She would come to no harm, of course. He knew that. But he could not help worrying about her anyway.

With a sigh that was both regret and anticipation he turned

and headed back toward the parlor of the old house. Any time now.

The mixture of feelings jelled into one—eagerness—as he heard the creak of a footstep on the short stairsteps leading to the porch that overlooked the water.

Lucy had barely had time to reach the turn onto the road. The little Ranger was not wasting any time.

Raider stopped in the hallway and waited for Tillman to join him.

A shadowy figure appeared in the door at the open end of the hall, outlined dimly against the starlit early night sky beyond.

There was something . . .

The man at the door was tall and burly!

Henry Thomas Tillman was short and slender.

Raider's hand swept the big Remington free, and he dropped to one knee, pressing himself against the wall at his side.

The figure in the doorway held a short, cut-down shotgun.

Raider had never known the little Ranger to use anything but his undersized revolver!

The man on the porch eased the screen door open silently and slipped inside carefully, moving on stockinged feet so as to make no sound on the bare wood flooring.

Behind Raider, from the direction of the parlor, there was a slight, scratching sound. As of a window frame being opened in stealth.

Raider smiled grimly, the expression close to being a grimace.

They had come. The sons of bitches had come for him.

They must have spotted him here over the weekend. Perhaps the pirates or someone connected with them had been in one of those innocent-seeming boats on the waterway when he and Lucy took the *Cockleshell* out for their picnic. Or perhaps . . .

It didn't matter.

The fact was that they had come.

Raider eased back the hammer of the Remington, holding it tight against his belly to muffle the sound of the sear engaging the hammer stops.

The man at the front was halfway down the hall now, only a matter of paces in front of Raider. He was unaware of the deadly presence of a defender in that same hallway. He moved cautiously forward, sliding his feet across the boards of the flooring instead of striding, so that he would make no noise.

He was still outlined against the dark gray of the night sky behind the complete blackness of the hallway, though.

He was only three yards away, two, practically at Raider's side now.

Raider wanted to take at least one of the pirates alive for questioning. But there were more of them outside the house. Or perhaps inside it by now. There was at least one other. Probably more. He had only seen or heard two, but there could well be a dozen of them.

He would take his chances at capturing another of them but first remove the threat of this one.

Raider extended his arm and came to his feet, the cartilage in his knees popping lightly as he did so.

The man was no longer in silhouette. He was too close for that. The angle of sight between hunter and hunted put the wall of the hallway behind him now.

"Wha . . . ?"

Raider fired, the muzzle flash of the Remington lighting the entire back end of the hall for a fraction of a second.

The impression left in Raider's vision was like a photograph, yet a plate somehow taken in vivid color and capturing a frozen instant of time, as with a shutter a thousand times faster than any camera shutter ever yet devised.

The brief flash of light caught the pirate—Raider saw the man clearly enough to recognize and remember him from the *Henrietta*—with the shape of his head distorted, the head itself wrenched sideways to an unnatural angle, the curling hair over his temple flaring with sudden flame, his expression oddly calm as if he did not have time enough to realize that he was already dead.

Raider had killed before. But never like this. The eerie sight in the flicker of light from his own muzzle flash affected him. But he had no time to think of that now.

He was wheeling toward the parlor door, recocking the Remington, driving himself low and forward, even before the body of the dead man had time to thump with sickening finality onto the floorboards.

Raider *felt* movement from inside the parlor.

He couldn't hear it. Rather, he felt it, through the floor to the soles of his feet, through the wall he was leaning against now.

It occurred to him that he could hear nothing. He could not even consciously recall hearing the ear-shattering roar of a .44 cartridge fired in close confinement. He could hear nothing at all, but his nostrils were filled with the acid stench of burnt powder.

He shot his jaw and swallowed hurriedly, trying to break whatever the blockage was in his hearing.

A fight at night is conducted with the ears, not the eyes, as the principal outreach of the senses, and whoever was in the parlor now was not under the same disadvantage as Raider.

The parlor door swung open, and a hand holding a revolver was extended around the door frame, pointing toward the front of the house where the gunshot had come from.

Raider leveled the Remington not at the tiny, only vaguely seen target of gun and hand but at the lightly plastered wall just this side of the solid wooden doorjamb.

He fired again, and the hand and gun disappeared.

Damn it, this time he was conscious of the pressure against his eardrums. His ears hurt, and they rang dully, painfully, with a false impression of sound.

He stayed low and scuttled backward the length of the hall. There was another door there. It led to the kitchen lean-to that had been built onto the back of the boxy old house.

Again he felt rather than heard a heavy movement from inside the parlor. Something had fallen to the floor, the impact of it transmitting through the boards to Raider. A body falling? Or only a chair knocked over? He had no way of knowing.

He felt for the knob of the kitchen door, found it, then hesitated.

Moving with deliberate speed he shucked the two empties from the cylinder of the Remington and replaced them with fresh cartridges. He still had no idea how many men he faced. Or where they were.

A felt and distantly heard sound reached him as a gun was fired on the other side of the parlor wall. Bits of shattered lathing and plaster sprayed the wall near where he had been moments earlier.

At least one of them was alive and busy in there.

The .44 reloaded and ready again, Raider came to his feet,

twisted the knob of the kitchen door, and threw himself forward.

A man was standing at the outside door, on the small porch that covered the water barrels Estevan brought for the household's use.

This one too had a sawed-off shotgun in his hands, but he was taken by surprise when Raider bolted into sight.

The split second of shocked immobility was all he would ever get.

The Remington bucked in Raider's fist, and the man was flung backward out of the doorway, the shotgun falling from his hands and his arm-flailing, windmilling figure caught for a moment at the edge of the porch as he fought to retain his balance, then toppled out of sight.

That one was hit, Raider knew, but not yet dead.

If only he could hear! Hear something. Anything.

He closed the kitchen door behind him and bolted it shut. The light bolt would not keep out anyone who really wanted through, but it might grant him a delay of several seconds if anyone tried to take him from inside the house. That was all he could hope for. But a second's grace could mean all the difference when he was unable to hear the approach of someone at his back.

Damn! He pinched his nostrils shut, clamped his mouth firmly closed, and blew, trying to equalize the pressures inside his ears.

He felt-heard a slight pop. Perhaps there was some improvement. He couldn't be sure.

There were only the two doors off the kitchen. One into the central hallway that ran the length of the house. The other to the outside porch.

Both must surely be covered by now.

And below that porch there was a wounded pirate who Raider had to assume was still alive and armed.

Raider crouched low and moved forward.

He could see no one. He could hear nothing.

The shotgun dropped by the man on the porch was lying on the doorsill where the man had been entering when Raider shot him.

At close quarters, at night, there was no weapon that could compare with the deadly effect of a short-barreled shotgun.

Raider crept forward, alert to any movement outside the house.

He could see nothing. There had to be men out there. Had to be. But he couldn't see them.

Carefully, he sheltered behind the plank wall of the kitchen—the wall was too thin to offer much protection, but at least it would keep him from being seen—and retrieved the shotgun.

He crabbed backward across the sandy-gritty floorboards until he was well clear of the spot where he might have been seen, then broke the action of the double-barreled gun and checked the brass shell casings.

Both barrels were loaded. He had no way to determine what size shot was in those shells. But whatever it was it was something heavy enough for a pirate to use when hunting Raider. It would likely do.

With a grim smile, Raider earred back both hammers of the scattergun and dropped his Remington back into his holster. The two-shot gun was the better for what he needed right now.

A faint rattling reached his ears. His hearing seemed to be returning, at least a little. Outside, the moon must have broken free of the clouds, because now there was enough light coming through the kitchen windows that he could see the door to the hallway quiver and catch against the bolt.

Raider shifted forward a few feet, moving in what he hoped was silence, and lay flat on the hard boards, facing the door and aiming the deadly shotgun straight down the hallway beyond it.

If anyone was in that hall when the door sprang open . . .

The door jiggled again, then stopped.

Raider knew what was coming.

From *both* directions, probably. If these SOBs had any sense, then certainly.

He waited, steeling himself against the shock that had frozen the man he surprised when he burst into the kitchen minutes earlier.

There was a moment of quiet.

Then the kitchen door burst wide, flying back on its hinges and rebounding against the wall.

Raider triggered the first barrel, and a scythe of hot lead chopped into the bodies of the two men in the hallway.

Both went down screaming, but Raider had no time to think about them now.

He rolled, bringing the squat, ugly muzzles of the shotgun away from the hall and toward the porch.

A dark form appeared there, bounding up the steps to the porch, and then another.

Raider fired the second barrel, and both figures disappeared, swept backward in the blink of an eye.

Raider dropped the empty shotgun and palmed his Remington, returning his attention to the hall.

But the only men he could see there were crumpled on the floor, motionless now and for all time to come.

He swiveled back toward the porch, the .44 held ready, its muzzle weaving back and forth like the triangular head of a snake poised to strike.

There were no more targets.

Raider shot his jaw, swallowed, dug a fingertip into his ear. He honestly did not know if he could hear again or not.

There could have been men shouting beyond the walls that surrounded him. Or the night could have been empty and silent around him.

He backed into a corner where he would be protected from any fire through the walls by the bulk of the zinc sink.

And waited.

This, he knew, would be the hard part.

CHAPTER THIRTY-TWO

"You played hell, Rade."

"Yeah," he said listlessly. He dug a finger into his ear. It was past dawn, and even though an entire night had gone by since the attack, his hearing was still off.

The sound of Henry Thomas's voice reached him as though they were talking underwater or he had a head full of cobwebs that the sound had to filter through before he could grasp it.

In addition to everything else, he was tired. Lordy, but he was tired. He had spent the night in that corner with the Remington held ready and with an irrational conviction that the rest of them were going to burst through the doors at any moment.

He hadn't moved from from the spot until daybreak let him even the odds if they were still out there waiting for him.

And then there was only blood to see.

Blood and bodies.

A shotgun makes a helluva mess.

"Looks like you near wiped them out, Rade," Tillman went on. "Five bodies they left behind. And, shit, from the blood on the ground outside, I'd say the ones as weren't killed right off must've bled to death." Tillman smiled at him. "Sure do wish you'd learn to take some of 'em alive, though. I try and teach you, but it don't seem to do much good. Hardheaded son of a bitch." His smile, like his tone of voice, was friendly and understanding. Raider had had a bitch of a night.

"Sorry I wasn't here to get in on it," the little Ranger said. "I expected to be, of course, but I got delayed in Ingleside waiting for an answer to my telegrams."

"Well? Did we do any good there?"

Tillman shook his head. "It's just like we figured to start with. Just like with your ladyfriend's *Cockleshell*. The owner of the *Albacore Lady* tied up. Next time he looked, his boat was gone. He reported the loss right away." The Tall Man shook his head a second time but for a different reason. "Sure hope the poor fella had insurance. A lot of commercial fishermen don't. Figure they can't afford the fees, so they pin their futures on hope instead o' insurance companies."

"Like farmers," Raider said.

"The difference is, it don't cost no two, three thousand dollars for a plow."

Raider whistled. "I had no idea what a boat could cost."

"Hell, Rade, a fishing trawler is cheap. Try buying one of Jon Harwig's coasters. Worse, try and pick up a deepwater hull. Some of them can set you back fifty, even sixty thousand."

"That's a lot of money, Henry Thomas. More than enough to justify a touch of piracy."

"Sure. Except so far as anybody can figure out, not a one of those missing ships has ever turned up anyplace else."

"You've looked?"

"Damn right we've looked. And not just my pencil pushers in the Rangers, neither. Not all the Navy boys are stupid. I've asked *their* pencil pushers. And the Mexican navy too. I have some friends that side of the border. I put the word out before I ever started this job. Even had some friends check into registrations of new ships"—Raider remembered Morton Bell back in Mobile saying he had checked into that line of thinking too without success—"even new shipping companies being incorporated. Nothing. That's exactly what it all turned up. *Nada.*"

Raider glanced out the window toward the line of bodies he and Henry Thomas had dragged outside and lined up under the shelter of the carriage shed where they might not bloat so quick. "Those men weren't in this thing for fun," he said.

"No, there's profit in it someplace. Has to be."

"The cargoes haven't been all that valuable. Hell, a couple of the ships were carrying nothing but ballast when they were taken. And at his point poor Harwig isn't getting much in the way of valuable cargo anyhow."

"It confuses the hell out of me," Tillman admitted.

Raider rubbed at his eyes. They felt gritty and burning

from lack of sleep. From tension, too, if the truth be known. He had been almighty pleased to see Henry Thomas Tillman this morning and not a bunch more gunmen.

"Look, I guess what we better do is split up again. Those boys aren't going to get any sweeter-smelling by letting them lay there. I'll ride for town and get someone to come fetch the bodies for burial. Identification, too, if anybody knows them. Then . . ." He shrugged.

"We try it again?"

"They damn sure have reason to come after me now. If they didn't before so much and came anyway, well, they'll damn sure be wanting my ears pinned to the barn wall now."

Tillman smiled. "Get it straight, Rade. They'll want those jug ears of yours nailed to the mast, not a barn wall."

Raider was feeling too weary to be playful so he let it pass, even knowing that Tillman was only trying to make him feel better after a long hard night.

"Find yourself a place to stay out of sight," he said. "I'll be back this afternoon with a burial party. We'll see what happens after that."

Tillman nodded, and Raider headed out to the shed where the ugly blue roan was tied.

CHAPTER THIRTY-THREE

Jon Harwig was ecstatic. "You've broken their back, Raider. Thank God, sir. You've destroyed them." He grabbed Raider's hand in both of his and pumped Raider's whole arm in his effort to offer both thanks and congratulations.

"I hate to bust your bubble, Jon, but all I've done is to thin the ranks. The captain wasn't among the dead. Whoever the man is and whatever he's up to, he's still out there someplace."

"But they've been devastated, Raider. Surely you can see that. Besides, sir, seamen are an honest lot. Believe me, it won't be easy for that captain or anyone else to find men willing to commit piracy." Harwig was grinning and still shaking Raider's hand.

"If you say so," Raider said dubiously. Perhaps Jon Harwig believed the job as good as ended, but Raider did not.

He turned the bodies over to Marshal Dowling and nodded across the mass of heads of the gathered crowd toward where Lucy Barnes was waiting for him on the sidewalk. Lucy looked as nervous as Harwig was excited.

As soon as she saw that he was free of the press of onlookers she turned and walked quickly back toward the chandlery, with Raider trailing behind at a discreet distance.

She was waiting for him immediately inside the doors, though, the huge store empty except for the elderly clerk, Wallace. The attention of virtually everyone else in town was down the main street, around the wagonload of bodies Raider had brought in.

As soon as they were alone Lucy flung herself into

Raider's arms, her lips seeking his while her hands roamed quick and hard up and down the length of him, grasping at his biceps, ranging over his chest and sides, touching and clutching swiftly as if to assure herself that he was there, all still together, unharmed.

"Whoa," he said, laughing. "Calm down."

"I . . . I can't. I know it's silly, but . . . when I heard you'd been in a fight . . . that there were men dead . . . you should've stopped here before you went back to the house, dear. I know you were in a hurry, but . . . I would have felt ever so much better if I could have seen you. Just for a moment. Just for a glimpse of you. To know that you were well." She was speaking in a breathless rush and all the while touching and prodding and seeing for herself that he was unwounded.

Raider laughed again and swept her into his arms, guiding her toward the staircase that led to the privacy of her office upstairs.

On the far side of the merchandise-cluttered room Wallace coughed into his fist and looked away.

Raider tugged his boots on and stamped his feet into them, then buckled his gunbelt back in place. Sometime since he was here last Lucy had had a leather-covered sofa brought into the office. It made for more comfort if less excitement in the moments they had together here.

"You look sad," he said.

Lucy turned away from him, fiddling with the buttons at the front of her dress. "I was just thinking . . . now you'll be leaving. I shan't see you again."

"Why would you think that?" he asked, genuinely puzzled.

"But I heard . . . after you were here to get the wagon and left again . . . I heard that the pirate gang was broken. That your job here was done. I naturally assumed . . ."

Raider smiled at her. "And so everyone believes, dear. Harwig included. The truth is that I'm far from being done."

"But with the pirates all dead now . . ."

He shook his head. "Not all of them, honey. Probably not half of them. And their leader wasn't among those dead. Remember, I saw their captain when they took the *Henrietta*. The leader wasn't among the dead ones. This thing isn't over."

Lucy's eyes widened. She looked worried.

"What is it, honey? I thought you'd be glad that I'd be staying."

She blinked. "I am, dear. Truly I am. But that means you're still in danger from them. It means . . . they shall still be wanting to hurt you, dear."

Raider laughed and pulled her to him. He held her close and rocked her slowly back and forth inside the protective circle of his arms. "Is that what's worrying you now? Shee-uh-oot, ma'am. I thought you'd've figured that out by now. I'm a tough old bird and not so easy to put down. Don't you be worrying about me, honey. If you have to worry about anybody, do it for the pirates that got away last night. They're the ones that need somebody's fears."

"Don't, Raider dear. You frighten me when you talk like that."

"Aw, honey, I wouldn't wanta scare you for anything." He kissed her. After a time she relaxed and grew calm again.

CHAPTER THIRTY-FOUR

"Why, you damn little ghoul," Raider said when he got back to the beach house that evening. "You been grave robbing."

Henry Thomas Tillman gave him a look of haughty dignity. "Please. I've been body picking, not grave robbing. There *is* a difference."

Raider looked at the pile of articles jumbled on the top of Lucy's dining room table. "Huh!" he said. "I know what it is. You finally decided to carry a man-sized weapon. Give up that toy of yours and start toting a shotgun. Good."

"Actually," Tillman said, sobering, "there's some interesting stuff came out of the pockets of those pirates. Take a closer look."

Raider shrugged and fingered through the small items that had come out of the pockets of the dead. It all seemed perfectly ordinary. Coins, both silver and gold in small denominations. Several pocketknives. One bandanna handkerchief. Two keys, both small and therefore intended for padlocks or trunks rather than doors. Two largish nails with the ends flattened to a spoonlike shape and then bent into a curve, the flat ends showing traces of mud. A black pebble smoothed and polished from being long carried or handled and almost certainly a good luck piece. One token redeemable for a short-time at a whorehouse called La Paloma Negra. Fourteen dollars in folding currency. And finally, incongruous here considering its source, a much thumbed pocket-sized New Testament with a badly worn cover and an inscription that read: "Jimmy, With love, Mother, September 9, 1873."

Raider looked through it all dutifully but had to turn to

Tillman with a shrug when he was done. "If you say it's interesting, Henry Thomas, I'll have to take your word for that, but to tell you the truth it all looks like the usual old shit to me."

The little Ranger grinned and gave Raider a superior look. He pulled a chair out and hunched over the table. "You don't see it, do you?"

"I don't see it," Raider agreed.

"Sit down, an' look here, landlubber."

Raider sat, although he damn sure didn't understand why.

"Now think about this," Henry Thomas said. "We looked those bodies over. No spurs this time, of course. But those boys was wearing boots, and those boots showed where spurs had been strapped to 'em real often."

"Sure, but we both of us noticed that right off. I remember you remarking it just this morning. Naturally a man who's trying to make a sneak on somebody at night might think to pull his spurs."

"Right," Henry Thomas said. "But while you was gone, I took a closer look at the bodies. Those boys showed wear on the insides of their britches, where a man would grip with his thighs when he's riding a horse."

"We already figured that much from the fella we dropped outa that pecan tree," Raider said.

"Sure. But this is more than just more of the same, Rade." Tillman reached over and pulled to him the pocketknives and the two flattened nails. He handed Raider one of the nails first. "What would you say this is?"

"It's a hoof pick, of course."

Tillman grinned. "Of course. It's a hoof pick. Common, ordinary, everyday ol' thing. Right?"

"Right." Raider still didn't see what Henry Thomas was getting at.

"Now take a look at these knives. Look at each of 'em close."

Raider did as the little man wanted, although it made no sense to him. Still, he humored the Ranger and examined each of the three knives. They were all folding pocketknives, as common as dirt and available cheap in just about any store Raider could think of. One of the three had a single blade, the other two were two-blade folding knives. Each of them showed pocket wear on their handles and some degree of use and sharpening on the blades.

"So?"

"Those blades," Henry Thomas said, as if they were significant of something.

Raider shrugged again. "Those blades, shit. They're plain ol' blades. Sharp enough to whittle a stick but not so sharp you could shave with 'em. What of it?"

Tillman chuckled. "Look at this one. What are those blades?"

Raider was about to get irritated, but he humored the little man one more time. "Just what I said. Plain ol' knife blades. One cutting blade. One sheepsfoot that's a whole lot sharper than the big blade."

"My point exactly," Tillman exclaimed.

"Have you lost your damn mind, Henry Thomas?" Raider was running out of patience.

"But don't you see it, Raider? No, I expect you don't. You haven't spent all that much time around boats, so of course you wouldn't."

"You're going to have to explain it to me, whatever this grand discovery of yours is."

"What does a man use a sheepsfoot blade for, Rade? Close, extra-sharp cutting, mostly. Cutting leather, mostly. Or castrating. A sheepsfoot is even called a nut blade, some places."

Raider blinked.

"Which is all interesting enough. But there's something you *don't* see in any one of these knives, Rade. Something that you ought to see but that isn't there. And as a landlubber, you wouldn't likely notice it."

Tillman pulled out his own pocketknife and laid it in front of Raider. It too was a common, quite ordinary two-bladed knife. But with a difference. There was a primary cutting blade. And instead of a second knife blade, there was a small, sharply pointed awl as the second "blade."

"That," Henry Thomas Tillman said, "is a pocketknife a seaman would carry."

"Because of the awl," Raider guessed.

"Exactly. A stockman doesn't need an awl. If he's working leather and wants to make a hole, he mostly uses a punch anyhow. An awl only if there's no punch handy, and for emergency use a knife tip will do the job. He doesn't really need an awl in his pocket all the time. He breaks a catch rope, he throws the son of a bitch away and makes him a new one off the spool you'll find in every tack shed, right?"

"Sure," Raider agreed.

"But a sailor, a seaman, he looks at rope different. A rope that's broken or one that's frayed, that sort of thing can kill him. The wrong sheet or line parting, that can actually kill him and every other man aboard ship. So seamen are careful of ropes. They live by them and they play with them. A sailor sees a weak spot in a rope, he splices the thing. And he uses an awl like mine, if he hasn't anything better to hand, to separate the cable strands of the rope he's working on. Now me, I use the awl on this knife as a hoof pick when I'm working and to work with ropes when I'm on my boat playing. But not one of these dead pirates had anything on them that I'd associate with a seaman. Not a one of them." Tillman leaned back and nodded abruptly, as if to affirm to Raider the certainly of what he was saying.

"One thing more, Rade. There isn't a bit of knot work in the pockets of any one of those dead boys. Not a thing. And sailors, they love knots. The fancier and more complicated, the better. A seaman is likely to carry bits of knotted cord to show off, if he's tied it himself, or to try and figure out, if it's been given to him. He's apt to wear necklaces or bracelets of fancy knot-work. But somewhere on or about him, he's just damn sure likely to have some show-off knots. And there isn't a thing like that anyplace on this table."

"What you are telling me," Raider said, "is that these boys really don't have much to do with the sea. Except maybe when they're busy pirating Jon Harwig's ships."

Tillman grinned. "That is *exactly* what I am telling you, Rade. We already had it under our noses after we saw the boots and spurs on that first body. Now these guys as much as rub our noses in the obvious. What the evidence suggests, Rade, is that these pirates don't have shit to do with the sea or ships. They're a bunch of *cowboys*, for cryin' out loud. A bunch of damn cowboys!"

"Now why in hell would a bunch of cowboys turn to pirating for a hobby?" Raider mused out loud.

Henry Thomas Tillman grinned again. "I already did the hard part, Rade. Now you can figure out the rest of it."

CHAPTER THIRTY-FIVE

They had a lead. It might or might not mean anything, but Henry Thomas said he knew of La Paloma Negra. He said that at considerable risk—justly realized, as it turned out—that Raider would jaw him about the fact of a married man having knowledge of a cow-town whorehouse.

La Paloma Negra was a popular recreation spot in the vicinity of Refugio, almost directly inland from Rockport and the shallow waters of Copano Bay, which lay behind the peninsula where Rockport had been situated.

"Cow country?" Raider asked.

"As much so as anyplace in this part of the country. Mostly small spreads, not like the King outfit to the south. Good country. Good folks mostly, though there are some who like to slip out of the Brasada and find their fun at Refugio or Beeville or civilized places like that."

Raider knew about the Brasada. It was the thick, thorny country between the Nueces and Rio Grande rivers that had long been under dispute between the United States and Mexico. Perhaps as a result of that—combined with the difficult nature of the country itself—it was a hellhole and hideout for outlaws from both sides of the border, as wild if not as infamous as the Hole in the Wall territory far to the north.

"So you figure our pirates could be out of the Brasada?"

Tillman shrugged. "It's a possibility. We'll ask."

"Just waltz in there and start questioning folks?"

Henry Thomas looked at his friend—had to look up to do it, not only because of the relative size of the two men but because the sawed-off Ranger's mule was a good hand shorter

155

than Raider's homely blue roan as well—and grinned. "You Pinkertons get too used to the idea that you gotta do things on the sneak, Rade. You forget, I got a badge tucked away in my knickers. Down in this part of the country, people tend to act polite when a Texas Ranger says he wants to have a quiet word with them." The grin got wider. "Wait an' see. Miz Maybelle Brewster is gonna be *real* anxious to give us all the help she can. If she doesn't, Miz Maybelle will be out of business inside a week, and I don't think she'll want that to happen."

Tillman's tone of voice said that he damn well meant it, too. About all Raider had seen of the Ranger before now was a smiling, easygoing, genuinely pleasant little companion.

But there seemed to be steel under Henry Thomas Tillman's mild exterior.

"I'll let you handle it, then," Raider said.

"Do that, friend. You just do that."

It took them a day and a half to reach La Paloma Negra. Decent mounts could have made the trip in a single day. But then, they did not have decent mounts, only the bony things Raider had been able to pick up in Rockport.

They arrived shortly before noon. The whorehouse, set in an oak grove a mile or more out of town, looked empty and lifeless behind tight-closed shutters. Come dark, Raider knew, there would be life aplenty behind those shutters.

They tied their animals out front, and Henry Thomas Tillman bashed on the front door loud enough to rouse a houseful of opium addicts. Even so they had quite a while to wait before finally they heard a complaining voice from inside.

"Keep 'em buttoned, damn it, you oughta know we ain't open fer no bizness yet."

There was a creaking of floorboards as the voice came closer, and Henry Thomas whammed the door again with his fist.

"I tolt you—" the voice from inside whined.

"And I'm telling you to open this door right fucking now, or I'll break the sonuvabitch down."

"Who . . . ?" A small judas set into the stout door was pulled open, and a pair of large brown eyes surrounded by shiny brown flesh peered out. The eyes got wide when they saw who the caller was, and quickly there was the sound of a bolt being drawn and a chain being dropped.

"Sar'nt Tillman. Do come inside, please."

Raider stifled a smirk. Henry Thomas had admitted to knowing the place. He had said nothing about having been a visitor here before.

Henry Thomas waited for the door to be opened, then stalked inside like an emperor entering one of his lesser possessions. Raider trailed silently behind him.

The little Ranger did not bother to introduce Raider to Mrs. Maybelle Brewster, but did point a finger at the heavyset Negro woman who had answered the knock and say, "This rich bag of lard is La Paloma Negra in the flesh." He wrinkled his nose like he found the thought of that flesh particularly distasteful. "If she offers one of her girls to you, you better pass. They're all a bunch of damn douchebags, and they carry every disease known to man. Maybe invented some, for all I know." He said it to Raider but continued to scowl at the madame of the brothel while he spoke.

"Now, Sar'nt, you *know* I run the cleanest house in the south o' Texas, Sar'nt. You *know* that," the obviously frightened woman protested. "My girls every one of them is clean as new snow, an' you've never heard oncet about any cowboy bein' robbed or harmed any way in my place. Now why you come here botherin' me like this, an' me a simple workin' lady trying t' make her way?"

Henry Thomas Tillman dropped his hardnosed act and chuckled, reaching up to pat Mrs. Maybelle Brewster on her ample cheek. "Are you gonna ask us to lunch, Miz Maybelle? We've come a long way and haven't eaten yet."

Mrs. Brewster looked relieved. She smiled and ushered them toward the back of the house, into a kitchen that was plain and efficient, unlike the front of the place, which was furnished in garishly over-plush velvet and brocade.

There was no sign of the working girls—they were probably all still asleep at this midday hour—but the cook was awake and building a fire in the huge range.

Mrs. Brewster took charge of providing them with coffee and a vast lunch, then shooed the cook's ears away from the kitchen before she got around to asking them their business.

"Anything you need, Sar'nt. Anything at all. You know I'm always pleased to be able to help the gennelmen o' the law."

"I know you are, Miz Maybelle," Henry Thomas said, his

concentration on a platter of fried chicken in front of him. "My friend here is going to describe some boys we need to talk to. You tell us who they are and where we can find them, and we won't be bothering you any further."

Mrs. Brewster hesitated for a moment, obviously torn between self-interest and a sense of loyalty to her customers.

"It's important, Maybelle," Henry Thomas said. His voice was soft, but there was that hint of steel again in an undertone.

"You ask me whatever you want, Ranger," she said to Raider. She seemed to be under the impression that he too carried a badge. It was not an impression that either he or Henry Thomas Tillman saw fit to correct.

Raider described the pirates he had seen on the *Henrietta*, concentrating mostly on their leader, and was able to give fuller descriptions of the dead men.

"An' what'd you say you wanted with those boys?" Mrs. Brewster asked when he was done.

Raider opened his mouth to speak, but Tillman snapped out an answer first. "You don't ask that, Maybelle." The steel was definitely back in his voice now.

"Of course. Of course." Mrs. Brewster wrung her hands for a moment, but she had no choice about it and everyone knew it.

"The gennelmen you want to see belong over to the Y Box 3 outfit. You know them, Sar'nt?"

"Never heard of them."

"The brand's Y Box 3, like I say, an' the foreman is Nate Simms. He'd be the gennelman you first tolt me about. But I haven't seen Mr. Nate here in an awful long time. Used to come regular, but I haven't seen him in, oh, near a year. His boys still come, though. That would be the rest of the gennelmen you say you want to, um, talk with. It's only eighteen, twenty miles over t' the Y Box 3. Or so I believe. I never been there, you understand. Never had no reason to go out lookin' for my clients." She smiled, but neither Raider nor Tillman allowed their own expressions to soften.

"You say this Simms is the foreman," Raider said. "Who owns the Y Box 3?"

"Oh, I wouldn't be knowin' that. I jus' know Mr. Nate is the foreman. No idea who the owner would be."

Tillman grunted. "Do you know exactly where this place is?"

The woman shook her head quickly. "Not really. Just that it's far enough out that they can't come in, like, easy after a day's work. But near enough that they c'n come regular on the weekends. Like I say, twenty miles at a guess. I have that idear, anyhow. I could be wrong. Never had reason to ask."

"We can find out," Tillman said coldly. "We can also find out if anybody out there has been tipped that some Rangers want to have a word with them."

"You know me better'n that, Sergeant."

"I know you, Maybelle. That's why I'm reminding you. You keep your mouth shut about this. Otherwise..." He didn't finish the sentence. He didn't have to.

There was a gray, ashen look under the rich brown of Mrs. Brewster's skin. "You gennelmen enjoy your dinner, hear? I'm gonna go freshen up an' put my face on. Be gettin' callers any time now." It would be hours yet before any customers showed up at the whorehouse door, but Raider and Tillman ignored the nervous madame's lie.

She bustled out of the kitchen, leaving them alone with an excellent meal. Raider was ready to leave, but Henry Thomas Tillman insisted on staying until they had eaten.

"After all," he said, "it'd be a shame to let it go to waste." He smiled at Raider and dug into the chicken and freshly baked biscuits.

CHAPTER THIRTY-SIX

It was Henry Thomas Tillman's fault that it took them so damned long to get there.

Raider's preference would have been to march straight out to the Y Box 3 and commence raising hell. Henry Thomas Tillman saw it otherwise, and somehow the little Ranger had more or less taken over ever since they approached La Paloma Negra.

Tillman insisted on going first to the courthouse to prowl through the public records.

For whatever it was worth, they now knew that the Y Box 3 was owned by an outfit registered as the L & L Land and Cattle Company, that it had been bought—probably on the cheap—during the lean postwar years, that the taxes had lapsed shortly thereafter but were picked up and paid in full after an interval of some years, that in recent times all brand registrations and other documents had been signed by Nathan Simms on behalf of the legal owners and that the company paid taxes on 7,042 acres of deeded land, 613 head of breeding cattle (suckling calves and steers under the age of two excepted from the tally), and 3,414 sheep. The Y Box 3 was definitely no front. It was a working and paying proposition for its owners.

While Henry Thomas Tillman—Sergeant Tillman, that is —had been gathering all that presumably valuable information, Raider made himself useful by finding out just where the damn place was, which was really his only interest in the courthouse records.

Raider admitted to himself, though, that the Tall Man was

interested in building a case that he could take before a prose-
cuting attorney. Raider was only interested in nabbing the sons
of bitches. It would be someone else's affair to play the court-
room games.

Thanks to what Raider considered an old-maidish flaw in
Henry Thomas Tillman's character, it was well past dark before the sorry mule and even sorrier blue roan got them within
sight of the lights of the Y Box 3.

"'Bout damn time," Raider grumbled.

"Oh, hush. If we'd gotten here any earlier they woulda all
been out working anyhow," Tillman said.

Raider would have complained about that observation too
except that it was probably true. Maybe the little fart had been
thinking after all.

"Now what?" Raider asked, drawing the choppy-gaited
roan to a merciful halt.

Henry Thomas grinned at him. "Now we knock on the
door an' start earning our pay, Rade."

"Just walk in and arrest them?"

The little man's grin got bigger. "Exactly." Tillman booted
the mule forward, tossing over his shoulder, "I sure as hell
don't know why we didn't think to borrow some decent horses
when we were in town, though."

Raider agreed with that completely.

There was a small ranch house among the many buildings
of the Y Box 3 headquarters, probably the foreman's house
now, but it was in a so-so state of repair and no lights showed
at its shuttered and unglazed windows. All the activity seemed
to be in a long, low bunkhouse where lamp oil was being
burned as though it had no value.

Henry Thomas Tillman rode in as bold and open as if he
had a personal invitation to the party and took his time about
tying the miserable mule at a hitch rail that was otherwise
empty.

Raider was feeling more cautious and held back in the
shadows until Tillman motioned him forward.

"Since I have the badge," the Ranger said, not bothering to
lower his voice in the least, "I'll knock at the door. If you feel
like it, Rade, you might want to mosey around back." He
grinned. "Just in case there's a back door to this snakepit."

Raider smiled. He'd been beginning to think that the little
fellow wasn't taking this crowd seriously. Not so. The

little guy was as brassy as the proverbial monkey's balls, but he wasn't stupid.

"I'll give you a minute to get there before I let the boys know that they're to line up for handcuffs," Tillman said with another grin. But still not in a soft voice, much less a whisper.

"You wanta blow a bugle too, t' let them know we're surrounding 'em. Or do you just like a good challenge."

Tillman laughed, loudly, and Raider hurried off toward the back of the bunkhouse before the idjit got any noisier.

A moment later and Raider got over his concern with Henry Thomas's noisemaking. There was a woodpile that he didn't see in the darkness, and he tripped over a stack of stovelengths with enough pure loud noise that he should have been heard over a drum and bugle corps on the Fourth of July, but no one inside seemed to pay any attention at all.

So much for sneakiness.

He took up a position by the back door and palmed his .44.

Over on the other side of the place Tillman must have been knocking, because all of a sudden the voices from inside went quiet and someone called out, "Come in."

Raider had done this sort of thing probably a hundred times before, but still he felt his shoulders hunch with tension. He leaned closer to an open window so he could hear better.

There were the small sounds of shuffling feet and then the creak of door hinges.

"Good evenin', boys."

"Yeah?"

"My name is Tillman, gentlemen. Henry Thomas Tillman, sergeant, Company F, Texas Rangers. You boys are all hereby detained for questioning about alleged felony charges, and—"

There was a scramble and some loud cussing, and hell began to pop.

A body came flying through the window beside Raider, smack through the paper blind that had been pulled down over the opening. Raider reacted without conscious thought, the heavy barrel of the Remington sweeping up to slash across the Adam's apple of the fleeing cowboy, dropping the man gagging into the dirt and putting that one at least out of commission for some time to come.

The window was open and uncovered then, so Raider thumbed back the hammer of the .44 and leaned over the windowsill.

Henry Thomas Tillman was inside the bunkhouse, standing with the log wall at his back and that pipsqueak little nickel-plated revolver of his extended at arm's length.

A Colt .45 bellowed, and splinters flew beside Tillman's ear while the little man took his aim.

The .32 Smith and Wesson spat, its sound small and almost polite compared to the roar of the bigger Colt, and a man crumpled to the floor.

Another cowboy—pirate; Raider recognized the man from the *Henrietta*—was over at the end of the room clutching a shotgun that he had just grabbed off a rack of the things. He looked like he was going to cut down on the Ranger, so Raider put a slug in his brisket and he lost interest in that task.

Everybody was grabbing for guns by then, and things got pretty brisk.

Someone tried to shoot out the overhead lamp, and Raider dropped him.

Tillman fired twice in rapid succession, and a pair of the cowboy pirates went down.

A tall man who looked vaguely familiar bolted through the back door with a shotgun swinging in search of a target, and Raider had to move fast to leave the windowframe, twist, and put a bullet into the man's guts.

The air was thick with the smell of burnt-powder smoke, and off in one corner an overturned table lamp was spreading oil and flame onto the dirt floor.

But just about as quick as the excitement started, it was over.

There were no more gunshots inside, but there was much moaning going on.

This time they had prisoners, by damn.

Raider looked in through the open window to see only two cowboys still on their feet, their weapons deposited on the floor in front of them and hands held high. Henry Thomas Tillman was holding them under the muzzle of his shiny revolver and was already reaching for his manacles.

Raider picked up the still gagging man whose throat was not feeling particularly well and muscled the lanky cowboy in through the back door.

"Got another customer for you," he told the little Ranger.

Henry Thomas nodded and said, "Do me a favor."

"Sure."

"Hold these boys under the gun a minute, would you?"

Raider nodded, shoved the cowboy in his grip toward the other two, and pulled his .44 again.

Once Raider had all three of them under his Remington, Henry Thomas grinned and snapped open the breaktop action of his Smith and Wesson. He shucked six empties onto the floor and carefully reloaded the revolver.

Raider got something of a kick out of the look on the faces of the two men Tillman had been threatening with the thing. The Smith had been empty as a whore's heart, and if the cowboy pirates had known it they could have cut Tillman to pieces.

One of them cussed, but by then it was much too late.

"Turn around, gentlemen, and I'll fit you for your new bracelets."

Muttering and bitching, the cowboys did as they were told.

CHAPTER THIRTY-SEVEN

"Damn it. Damn it, damn it, *damn* it!" Henry Thomas said.

"You'd think I did it on purpose," Raider complained.

"Oh, hell, I know you didn't. But damn it anyhow."

Raider shrugged. The damage was done, and there was no undoing it. The man who had come busting out the back door and who went down under Raider's bullet had been the pirate captain and ranch foreman Nate Simms. And there was damn sure no talking to him now.

What they had instead was four live prisoners, two of them wounded although not seriously, and a collection of corpses. Two of the dead men and one of the freshly wounded showed other recent wounds from Raider's slugs during the attack on the beach house.

This was the right crowd, all right. Raider remembered several of them, the dead Simms in particular.

With four live ones to talk to they should have been all right, except that the cowboys claimed that they knew damn little about the piracy.

"We're no damn sailors, see," one of them said, picking at a bandage that had been tied around his calf. "But the money was too good to pass. Nate'd learned how to sail, see, never said who taught him, but he was gone most of a month one time, an' he taught us. Not enough so's we could make out as sailors, which I fer one wouldn't wanta do even if I could, but enough that we could handle a boat or a ship long enough t' get the job done. 'Tisn't so hard if you put yer mind to it. Not like learnin' to stick with a bad horse or learnin' t' throw a brush loop."

"Now that you mentioned it," Raider said, "what the fuck was the job?"

"Whatcha mean? We was stealing ships, man. I thought you knew that." The cowboy seemed genuinely puzzled, and Raider decided the man hadn't necessarily been at the front of the line when brains were being apportioned.

"Yes," Raider said patiently. "But what did you *do* with the ships? After you stole them, I mean?"

"Oh, that." The cowboy grinned, exposing yellow stumps where teeth should have been. He laughed. "We sunk 'em."

"You what!"

"We sunk 'em. Didn't we, Danny?"

Danny, who was unwounded but dazed and seemingly in a state of mild shock to find himself in irons, nodded.

"Why in the hell would you steal a ship and then turn around and sink it?"

The first man shrugged. "Fer two hundred dollars a job, that's why. 'Cause we was told to sink 'em after we stole 'em, that's why. Shit, I dunno. Nate told us to sink 'em, so we sunk 'em."

"Can you show us where?" Tillman asked.

"Oh, sure. That's easy. We always took 'em to the same place to sink 'em. Whatever boys wasn't on that job with the rest of us'd be waiting there with horses so's we could get home."

"And the cargoes?" Raider asked. "What did you do with the cargoes?"

"Cargoes? I don't know nothing about cargoes."

"We never messed with whatever was downstairs," Danny put in, showing some interest in the conversation for the first time. "We never touched any of that stuff. Whatever was downstairs, we didn't have no truck with it."

"You scuttled the cargoes, too?" Henry Thomas asked.

"What's that word mean?"

"You sank the cargoes along with the ships?"

"Oh. Yeah. We never looked downstairs much. Except once when one of the boys found some cases of bottled-in-bond whiskey. We took that with us. Nate said it'd be okay."

"Of course." Henry Thomas made a face.

"Look," Danny said, "we're being cooperative. You know what I mean? You'll tell the judge about that, won't you?"

Tillman gave the cowboy a cold glare. "Maybe. It depends

on just how cooperative you stay. Piracy is a heavy rap, though. A hanging offense. I doubt a little cooperation will—"

"*Hanging*! Jesus Christ, man, y' only get two, three years for a stagecoach robbery. Why the hell should a ship robbery be any different!" Danny spurted to his feet, and Raider grabbed him by the shoulder—hard—and forcibly sat him back down again.

"It's a hanging offense," Raider confirmed. "Piracy doesn't come under regular law. It's under maritime law, and it's the rope for convicted pirates."

"Jesus!" Danny blurted again.

The third man, who was shot through the body and in considerable pain, began to cry, the shaking of his sobs aggravating the pain and turning him pale.

"Hanging," Tillman repeated in a sonorous tone. "By the neck. Until dead."

"That ain't fair," the first man wailed. "I went up fer knocking over a saloon once, an' I like to kilt the barkeep. Only got a year fer that, an' I was out in eight months. We never hurt nobody on them ships, so why should that be worse?"

"Because the law says it is," Raider said grimly. "And I don't think you get time off for good behavior when they hang you." He smiled at the frightened men. "Come to think of it, why were you so careful to not hurt anybody on those ships?"

The first cowboy shrugged. "Orders. Nate said that was real important, like. We wasn't t' hurt anybody or we'd get docked half our pay fer the job. So we never hurt nobody." He hadn't said it, but the implication was plain enough: if it hadn't been for those orders he couldn't have cared less if anyone was harmed or not.

The fourth man, who had been staring blankly off toward the front door and freedom, stirred and looked at his interrogators for the first time. "Shouldn't that count for something, sir? That we never harmed anyone? Surely they won't hang us."

"If you are convicted of piracy, you will hang," Henry Thomas said bluntly. "That is the law."

The fourth cowboy turned his gaze toward the door again.

"Who sent the ambushers after me?" Raider asked.

"Who're you?"

"Pinkerton operative."

"Oh, yeah. The fuckin' Pink."

Raider smiled into the man's face. "Right. The fucking Pink who's gonna be there to see you hang."

The cowboy paled.

"So who sent the ambushers after me?" Raider repeated.

"Nate. We got all our orders from Nate."

"And where did the deceased Mr. Simms get his orders?" Raider asked.

The man shrugged. "Dunno. Nate told us what t'do, an' he damn sure had the cash t' pay fer the jobs. That's all I know 'bout it."

Raider grunted.

"You said Nate was gone for a while. When he learned how to handle a ship. And then he came back and taught you. Did he have the idea for the piracy before that time or after?" the Tall Man asked.

The cowboy looked at Danny for a moment, as if that would refresh his memory. Then he said, "After, I think it was. Least I don't remember no talk about it before he took off that time."

"Is that right, Danny?"

"Yeah. Yeah, I think it was like that. After he took off."

"Where did he go when he left that time?"

The first man shrugged.

Danny said, "He never told us exactly. When he left he just said he was gonna go make a, uh, make a report. Something like that. We only figured he'd be gone a couple days, like he'd been before when he had to go off and do banking for the company or whatever. But I expect he got hooked up with whoever was paying for the jobs. So he sent a letter back saying he'd be gone a spell and for us to keep things running, that they was good for our wages and for Frank to take over until he got back."

"Frank?"

Danny pointed toward one of the corpses stacked in cord-wood fashion at the back of the place.

"Where did Nate go when he took those trips?"

"Rockport. But I don't know if that's where he was when he was putting this deal together. He never said."

Tillman shot a glance toward Raider, then turned back to the cowboy pirates. "Rockport?"

Danny nodded. "Sure. It's some jerkwater little place over on the coast. Or so I hear. I never been there myself, but my brothers used to trail cattle there for the hide market. That was back before there was a beef market up north. Used to piss me off because I was too little to go with them."

"You've never been to Rockport?"

"Nope. You, Len?"

The first cowboy, with the wound in his calf, shook his head. "Not that I recollect." He frowned in concentration. "No, I don't expect I have."

"But Nate used to go there?"

"Oh, yeah. Every few months he'd take off for a couple days, like Danny said."

"Do you know who he met there? Any of you?"

Each of them except the dazed man who was still silently weeping shook their head.

"No idea at all?"

"Nate never said."

"What kind of reports did Simms make on those trips?"

"About the ranch. Like that."

This time it was Raider who gave Henry Thomas a look. The unknown proprietor or proprietors of the L and L Land and Cattle Company? Probably. But there wasn't necessarily a connection between the ranch owner and the person or persons who had hired Nate Simms and crew for a spate of piracy.

"What made Simms think you boys would go for his suggestion that you become pirates?" Raider asked.

"I sure wisht you'd quit usin' that word, mister Pink. We done some robbing but we never pirated nobody."

"Taking a ship at sea is piracy under the law," Tillman injected. "Regardless of what you want to call it."

Len frowned.

"I asked why Simms would think this crew would go for piracy," Raider reminded them.

"Shit, man, we been pulling small jobs right along. You know. Knock over a greaser now an' then. Stick up a cattle buyer if one was handy. Like that. But that shit sure didn't pay out like the pi...uh...like robbin' ships. We pulled mighty good money fer that, let me tell you."

"Two hundred dollars a job, I believe you said?"

Len wistfully grinned at the fond memory of all that easy money. "Yeah. Two hunderd cash every time."

Tillman stood. "Do you have a wagon and team on the place?"

"Sure. Why?"

"I think it's time we transport you boys into town and put you behind some bars. Until time for your trial and hanging, that is."

"Please don't talk like that, damn it. We're doin' everything we can t' help."

"Sure you are. Just like you were doing everything you could to kill us just a little while ago."

Len turned his eyes away from the little Ranger's accusing stare.

Tillman went outside to find and hitch the team while Raider remained to keep an eye on the prisoners. Neither of them believed this crowd would be so easy to get along with if they had a chance to grab the upper hand.

CHAPTER THIRTY-EIGHT

They practically started a fistfight the next morning when they asked for a volunteer to show them where the Harwig ships had been scuttled. Each of the prisoners was anxious to be the one to show the most cooperation. It was a damn shame, Raider thought, that these boys knew so little, because they were sure all anxious to spill their guts about everything they did know—and whatever else they were capable of imagining.

Tillman finally chose the cowboy named Danny, since he was unwounded and probably the best of a poor lot when it came to what he had between his ears.

The others were turned over to Rangers from the Beeville barracks, and two Company D men rode with them to take charge of Danny when Tillman and Raider were done with him.

The place where the ships had been deliberately destroyed turned out to be in deep water off Cavallo Pass.

"All the ships and all the cargoes are out there?" Raider asked.

"Sure. Just like I said. We never took anything off them except that whiskey the one time."

"Not even the navigation instruments, expensive things like that?"

"I don't know about you, mister, but we never had any idea what was expensive and what wasn't. And we wouldn't of known where to fence ship stuff if we had known. Besides, Nate always said we wasn't to take anything that could show up later and tip somebody to us."

173

"How far out were the ships sunk?"

"Half mile. About that, anyhow."

"Is the water shallow enough that the ships or cargoes could be salvaged?"

"Now how the hell would I know a thing like that? I can't even swim, mister. Just looking at all this water makes me queasy to the stomach. Believe me, this sailing stuff is the shits."

"If you can't swim, how'd you get back onshore to the horses when those ships went down?"

"Aw, we was met. Some Mex in a boat met us. Nate'd sail around until the guy was there with the boat, then we'd set the ship to sinking and all come in on the boat to meet the boys who'd brought the horses." Danny hesitated for a moment. "Then we'd go, like, to McFaddin or someplace and have us a blowout with our pay for the job, then on back home."

"You got your pay on the spot?"

"Sure. Every time. The Mex with the boat had it for us. He handed it over to Nate, and Nate passed it on to us quick as we got to dry land again."

"Helluva payroll," Henry Thomas said.

"Yeah, I guess it was, especially since we all got paid the same. That way nobody got pissed if we had to stay behind and handle the horses or something."

"Helluva payroll," Tillman repeated. "And then to turn around and sink the ships and cargoes."

"It's a grudge thing, then, not profit." Raider said.

"So somebody has a real hard-on for Jon Harwig."

"Big, bad, and deep felt," Raider agreed.

"You're sure you never heard Simms say anything about who you were working for?"

"Believe me, Sergeant, if I knew anything I'd damn sure tell you. I . . . I don't wanta hang, Sergeant. And you promised you'd tell the judge I cooperated. You promised you'd do that, remember."

The Tall Man stared out to the Gulf, out toward the graveyard of half a dozen ships of the Harwig Line. He rubbed his chin. "Pity I have such a short memory. Sometimes I remember things. Sometimes I don't. Are you *sure* you don't know where Simms got his orders?"

Danny looked like he was going to weep. "I swear, Sergeant. I swear I don't."

Tillman ignored him. He motioned to the two privates from D Company and said, "Take this horse turd back to the pokey, where he belongs. There's people probably want him kept alive until the hanging. Though Lord knows I don't understand why." He turned to Raider. "You ready to head back to Rockport?"

"Yes." Raider sighed heavily. "It's time."

"You sound like you know something I don't, Rade."

Raider didn't answer. He reached under the roan's neck to flip the off rein over, then mounted. He barely spoke to Henry Thomas Tillman the rest of the day.

CHAPTER THIRTY-NINE

Henry Thomas Tillman had his pencil pushers. Well, Raider had something of the kind. He shot a wire off to Wagner in Chicago, another to Morton Bell in Mobile informing Gulf Insurance about the discovery of the ships and advising the insurors that the possibility of salvage might exist. Then he had a long talk with Jon Harwig and settled back to wait for the results of his Chicago inquiry.

Tillman got tired of pumping Raider for information that was not forthcoming from the suddenly tight-lipped Pinkerton operative.

"Look, damn it, this thing isn't over yet," Tillman insisted. "Nate Simms didn't go into the pirate business just for the hell of it, and nobody paid out that kind of money just as a practical joke on good old Jon Harwig. Somebody hates that man's guts, and they aren't going to quit preying on Harwig just because you and I kicked over the anthill and stomped all the ants that happened to be home at the time. If we back off this thing now, Harwig is still hanging out in the breeze, you know."

Raider agreed with everything the Ranger said but refused to add anything to the one-sided conversation.

"You do what you want, Henry Thomas. Me, I'm going to take a few days off to spend with Lucy."

Tillman looked like he was going to get huffy, but he managed to control himself. "You probably think you're putting one over on me, Raider, but I know you went to the telegraph office and got wires off to your home office and another to Gulf Insurance Company."

Raider smiled at him. "Know the contents of those wires, do you?"

"You know damn good and well I don't. Not the one I'm interested in, anyway. You sent the sonuvabitch in some kind of code."

For the first time in quite a while Raider grinned at the little man. Then he sobered. "Henry Thomas, I like you. I just naturally do. But I don't figure to say anything about what I got in mind until I know, I mean until I know for *sure* what's going on. Can you give me that much, Henry Thomas?" He hesitated, then added as if it were painful for him to get out. "Please?"

Tillman gave in and went away, muttering to himself.

It was Friday evening, and Raider hired the much despised blue roan again and rode south along the water to Lucy's beach house. He had agreed to meet her there and spend the weekend in her arms.

By the time he got back to Rockport Sunday night, or Monday morning at the very latest, the information from Wagner should be in hand. He would wrap it up then.

If he had the guts for it.

Raider wasn't entirely sure that he did, though, damn it.

"Darling!" Lucy was there ahead of him. She greeted him on the porch steps with a smile, a kiss, and a tall drink.

She took his arm to walk him up the steps and to a wooden armchair on the porch where she made sure he was comfortable and deposited the drink in his hand. He used his free hand to lightly stroke her thigh.

"La, dear. Not now. Someone might see." She softened the caution with another kiss. "Now *please* take the time to let me know you are all right, dear. You've been so terribly busy ever since you got back, but I've heard the most wonderful things. You did capture the pirates?"

"Those that weren't killed are in jail," he admitted.

"But that's wonderful, darling. I know Mr. Harwig must be pleased. Why, everyone in town seems to be thrilled with what you and that funny little man accomplished. Imagine him being a Ranger, though. I never would have guessed that. Just imagine."

"Oh, he is one all right. Pretty good man, too."

"He must be." She smiled at him fondly. "But not so good a man as you, I daresay."

Raider looked off toward the water. The *Cockleshell* was riding lightly on the waves at the dock.

Lucy noticed where his attention was. "I must give you that sailing lesson I promised, dear. Tomorrow morning?"

"That would be nice."

"Raider dear, you don't sound terribly enthused."

"What?" He blinked. "Oh. Sorry. My thoughts keep going elsewhere. My fault."

"Oh, I shall make you forget everything else, dear. Quite soon now. As soon as it's dark. We can go down by the water and make love under the stars. If you like, I can arrange some cushions in the cockpit of the boat. Doesn't that sound romantic? Making love to the rhythm of the sea?"

Raider winked at her. "Come to think of it, it does."

"As soon as it's dark, dear. Drink up now. I need to go in and see to supper, but I shall be back in no time. Then we can take that little walk down to the dock."

"Right."

Raider listened to Lucy's footsteps recede down the hall. It occurred to him that he never had gotten around to apologizing for the mess he had made of her beloved beach house. He hadn't even asked if there was any permanent damage.

He took a sip of his drink. She had certainly mixed it heavy enough. And she must have put some bitters in with the whiskey. He tasted it again. Not unpleasant, really.

He sighed and shoved his feet out, crossing his boots at the ankle and allowing himself to totally relax for the first time in days.

Damn, he thought.

Lucy returned to the porch a half hour later. The last hint of daylight lay pale to the west. There was a night sky over the Gulf to the east.

She stood in front of Raider and inspected him. He was slumped in the chair where she had left him, snoring softly. His glass, empty, lay on its side on the porch near the chair.

She smiled, looking even prettier when the pleasure softened her features.

"Estevan."

"Yes, señora?"

"You can come out now."

"Yes, señora."

The Mexican houseman, handyman, jack-of-all-trades came out onto the porch to join her. He was carrying a double-barrel shotgun, both barrels of which had been cut down to a vicious length.

"Don't just stand there, Estevan. Hand me the gun." She continued to smile down at Raider.

"Señora. Please. Would it not be better to let me take him out in the little boat? He would simply disappear. No one need ever know. Poof. He is gone. Jus' like the ships. Gone to the waves, señora."

"I already explained to you, Estevan. People in town know he came here. They would ask questions. Someone might suspect me. This way he is shot. I run screaming for help. The unknown leader of the pirates has made another attempt on his life, and this time they were successful. No, Estevan, it is much better if he is killed here on this porch." She smiled. "It is such a nice touch that this last threat to me should die on my daddy's porch, don't you think?"

Estevan did not answer, but he looked troubled.

"Hand me the gun, Estevan."

"Please, señora. No. This is not something you should do. If . . . if this man must die, at least, señora, please señora, allow me to be the one to kill him. For you. For your papa."

"Really, Estevan. You are being quite difficult. Now hand me that gun." Her patience was nearly exhausted. She stamped her foot prettily and held her hand out for the weapon.

"Señora. I insist. *Por favor.*"

"Damn you, Estevan!" She glared at the man for a moment, then relented. "Oh, all right. If it makes you feel any better."

"Thank you, señora. A thousand thanks."

"Just make sure you stand back a little ways. We don't want any powder burns on his clothing. That damned Ranger friend of his would never believe that anyone could have gotten close enough to leave powder burns and him not know it."

"Yes, señora. It shall be as you wish."

Estevan went down the steps into the sand and positioned himself in front of Raider and about a dozen feet away. "Is this far enough, señora?"

"I . . . I guess so. Hurry up now. That sleeping powder won't last forever, you know."

"Yes, señora." Estevan hesitated.

"What are you waiting for?" Lucy demanded.

"I think maybe I am too close still?"

"Then back up some more. But good heavens, Estevan, get it over with, will you?"

"Yes, señora." Estevan backed off two more paces. "I think you should move to the side, señora. It is said that these guns spread their bullets very wide."

"Shot," Raider said.

Estevan's eyes grew wide.

"Shot," Raider repeated. "Shotguns shoot shot, not bullets. And you're plenty far enough away to avoid powder burns." He sounded quite mild, even pleasant, as if explaining something to a child.

"But—"

"Aw, come on, Lucy. You think nobody's ever tried to slip me a mickey before?" He shook his head. "I sure as hell was hoping I was wrong about you, though, lady. I sure as hell was."

Estevan had been shocked into immobility by the sudden knowledge that Raider was not drugged. As the shock eased he reacted by clawing for the twin hammers of the double gun.

"Don't . . ." Raider started, but Estevan was too frightened to listen. He tried to aim the shotgun.

Raider's wrist moved with a motion so quick it seemed blurred, and his .44 spat lead and thunder.

Estevan dropped the shotgun and spun, dying even as he fell.

"Now, that's a shame," Raider said. "There are things I would've like to ask him."

Lucy's hands were clenched together. She pressed her knuckles against her full and very lovely underlip. "How did you . . . how did you know?"

Raider shrugged. "I can't say that I did know, Lucy. I guessed. And I hoped I was wrong. I sent wires to Chicago asking about the L and L Land and Cattle Company and, uh, about your maiden name, your parents, like that. But I sure was hoping those wires would come back empty."

"You bastard!" Lucy hissed.

"Probably. Just like you're a bitch. But you're sure a sweet one when you want to be."

"I loathed it every time I had to let you touch me, you bastard," Lucy swore.

"You wanted to keep track of what I was learning, right?"

"That is the *only* reason I would allow you to touch me."

Raider laughed. There was an undertone of bitterness in the sound, but he was able to get it out as a laugh. "Now you're funning me again, Lucy. You use your body just fine to get what you want. By the way, is that how you hooked Nate Simms on your pirate scheme? Did you fuck him until he never thought to realize that piracy is a hanging offense? I mean, Nate and his boys, they are—were—a low class of thieves, honey. Scared spitless of a gallows, every one of them. So I figure you probably fucked old Nate until his brains went to mush. Then he'd do anything you wanted."

"You are a vulgar, awful man, and I shan't allow you to speak to me in that manner."

"Now that's a good one, Lucy." He cocked his head and squinted, trying to see her better in the fading light. "Lucy Leonard, right?"

"That was my maiden name, yes. It is a name I am proud of."

"Sure. Lucille Leonard. Funny thing. When that ship's officer, McInally, was telling me about your daddy, he mentioned that Harwig'd had a partner named Leonard, but I figured that was the guy's first name. Then, oh, yesterday or thereabouts, I got to thinking that about everybody connected with this case had an L for an initial. And how McInally said that the ship he used to sail on, the one he'd been on when Harwig and your daddy had their fuss, how it was named the Something-or-other Lucille. And how your name was Lucille. And how it was during the heyday of the hide and tallow factories, back when your pa would have been riding high and rich, when that ranch was bought. You know. Things like that. They seemed to kinda fall together. You blaming Jon Harwig for your daddy's troubles. Like that. Though I still didn't want to believe it. Nope. Sure as hell didn't want to believe it."

"You cocksucker!" the delicate Mrs. Barnes snapped.

Raider smiled. "Honey, I've done a power of things, but that ain't among 'em. Besides, sticks and stones and all that bullshit."

"Don't use that kind of language in front of me, you bastard."

This time Raider's laugh was belly deep and the real thing. "Are you listening to yourself, Lucy? You ought to. You're a real card sometimes."

"What now, damn you? Will you shoot me down like you shot poor Estevan?"

"Aw, I feel bad enough about that already, Lucy. Poor guy was only trying to please you. Like every other man you get around. I figure he was the guy in the pick-up boat, wasn't he? The *Cockleshell*?"

She glared at him.

"How come you had to use your own boat that one time? Couldn't find one for the boys to steal? Or were you just tweaking people's noses, telling yourself how clever you were to pull all this off practically in front of everybody?"

Lucy refused to answer.

Raider sighed. "Anyhow, honey, in answer to your question, no, I expect I won't shoot you. Maybe I ought to, but I won't. Dying would be the kindest way out, of course. Even in Texas they won't likely hang a woman pirate. But you aren't gonna like spending the rest of your life behind bars."

He stood, shaking his head, and bent down to retrieve his hat. It had fallen onto the porch beside the deliberately emptied glass when he was faking sleep.

There was a flutter of cloth from where Lucy stood behind him, and he wondered if he was going to have to run the damn woman down and drag her all the way to town.

From twenty yards away, out in the deep shadows of the new-fallen night, there was a sharp crack of sound and a bright lance of flame.

Lucy cried out as Raider spun not toward the source of the gunshot but toward her.

She was holding a tiny Sharps four-barrel derringer clenched in both hands. He hadn't ever suspected she might have a pocket gun. The little weapon discharged harmlessly into the porch floor as her finger convulsed on the spur trigger.

Then she fell.

Even dying, he realized, the beautiful woman somehow

managed to drop to the floor with a lovely, swanlike grace. Like an actress on a stage pretending a death or a swoon.

The only thing marring the performance was the small, damp, scarlet dimple that had suddenly appeared in the center of her forehead.

"Jesus, Henry Thomas."

Tillman came forward. His hands were empty. There was no sign now of the deadly little .32 he carried.

"You didn't have to—"

"She was trying to kill you, Rade. I shot in a hurry. My aim was a little off. That's all." He looked Raider straight in the eyes when he said it.

"I—" Raider bit off the rest of what he had intended to say. He had seen Henry Thomas Tillman's abilities before. The little man had been trying to save more than Raider's life. He had saved the tall Pinkerton man from guilty regrets as well when he fired.

In a way, Raider appreciated what the little Ranger had done for him. In another way . . .

Raider shook his head. There was no point in going into it now. Nor later either, for that matter.

"Thanks," he said.

"Sure. Uh, are you all right?"

Raider nodded. "What the hell brought you out here, anyhow?"

Tillman gave him a thin smile. "You aren't the only one who knows how to send a telegram, you know. My pencil pushers in Austin had quicker access to the information than your people in Chicago. They got back to me this afternoon."

"Oh."

"Not so difficult to work out once we knew where to look, eh?"

"Yeah." Raider looked down at the body of the woman he had come so very close to. . . . He shook himself. Never mind *that* either.

"Let's head back to town, Rade," Tillman said gently, taking him by the arm and easing him away from the house. "We have some good news for Harwig, you know. And after we see him, why, I'll stand treat to the best damn tenderloin steak ol' Rockport has to offer."

Tillman guided Raider toward the horses. "Say, did I ever

tell you about the time . . . this was up toward Tascosa, mind
. . . about the time Tom Crawford and I got trapped in a buf-
falo wallow with a bunch of Comanche howling for our
scalps? Now let me tell you, Rade, that was a time. The way
it happened, see, was that . . ."

"THE MOST EXCITING WESTERN WRITER SINCE LOUIS L'AMOUR"
—JAKE LOGAN

_0-425-07700-4	CARNIVAL OF DEATH #33	$2.50
_0-425-07257-6	SAN JUAN SHOOTOUT #37	$2.50
_0-425-07114-6	THE VENGEANCE VALLEY #39	$2.75
_0-425-07386-6	COLORADO SILVER QUEEN #44	$2.50
_0-425-07790-X	THE BUFFALO SOLDIER #45	$2.50
_0-425-07785-3	THE GREAT JEWEL ROBBERY #46	$2.50
_0-425-07789-6	THE COCHISE COUNTY WAR #47	$2.50
_0-425-07974-0	THE COLORADO STING #50	$2.50
_0-425-08669-0	THE TINCUP RAILROAD WAR #55	$2.50
_0-425-07969-4	CARSON CITY COLT #56	$2.50
_0-425-08774-3	THE NORTHLAND MARAUDERS #60	$2.50
_0-425-08792-1	BLOOD IN THE BIG HATCHETS #61	$2.50
_0-425-09089-2	THE GENTLEMAN BRAWLER #62	$2.50
_0-425-09300-X	IRON TRAIL TO DEATH #64	$2.50
_0-425-09213-5	THE FORT WORTH CATTLE MYSTERY #65	$2.50
_0-425-09343-3	THE ALAMO TREASURE #66	$2.50
_0-425-09396-4	BREWER'S WAR #67	$2.50
_0-425-09480-4	THE SWINDLER'S TRAIL #68	$2.50
_0-425-09568-1	THE BLACK HILLS SHOWDOWN #69	$2.50
_0-425-09648-3	SAVAGE REVENGE #70	$2.50
_0-425-09713-7	TRAIN RIDE TO HELL #71	$2.50
_0-425-09784-6	THUNDER MOUNTAIN MASSACRE #72	$2.50
_0-425-09895-8	HELL ON THE POWDER RIVER #73	$2.75